Praise for *Visiting Hours*

"Few writers limn the numinous better than Jennifer
Anne Moses. Reading *Visiting Hours* I was swept up by the
searing, passionate visions haunting the unforgettable residents of Hope House, an AIDS hospice in Louisiana. With
an eye every bit as ruthless (at times) and penetrating as
Flannery O'Connor's, Jennifer Anne Moses yet manages to
orchestrate from the interconnected voices in this collection
of stories a chorale of grace and redemption.

Although she isn't afraid to pull out all the stops with the
fierce élan of a truly inspired writer, she is nonetheless a
meticulous craftsperson. Not only is her dialogue pitch perfect, but every descriptive sentence unfolds with perfect tim-
ing. I am in awe of her bravery, which allows her access to
the frontiers of perception and opens up another dimension
for today's fiction."

— James Wilcox, author of *Modern Baptists*

"Not tragic. Not comic. Not tragicomic, not melan-
choly, not any easy adjective - these stories, this place of
dreams and dying created by Jennifer Moses, left me moved
in very unexpected ways because of the utter originality of
her characters and their voices, and the singularity of their
dreams. Never met them before, and might never meet
them again, and that's what makes them unforgettable."

— Susan Straight, author of *Highwire Moon* and
Take One Candle Light a Room

VISITING HOURS

Jennifer Anne Moses

Fomite
Burlington, Vermont

ISBN-13: 978-1-937677-20-6

Library of Congress Control Number: 2012942156

Fomite
58 Peru Street
Burlington, VT 05401
www.fomitepress.com

Cover Art - Jennifer Anne Moses
Author Photo - Matt Grayson

Credits

"A Person's Happiness" was originally published as "Child of God" by *Glimmer Train* and appeared later in *New Stories from the South: The Year's Best.* "You Don't Know Nothing About Anything" originally apppeared in *Snake Nation Review.* "Jerome and the Angel" originally appeared in *Bryant Literary Review.* "Father Ralph's Vigil" originally appeared in *The Main Street Rag.* "Like a Sister" originally appeared in *Fiction.* "Blood Into Butterflies" originally apppeared in *Confrontation.*

This book is dedicated to my husband and True Love, Stuart Green

Awake, my soul! Awake, harp and lyre! I will awaken the dawn.
Psalms 57, verse 8

A PERSON'S HAPPINESS

When Gordon first laid eyes on Lucy he didn't think any-thing of her, skinny little white girl with a limp and that spaced-out, sideways-looking look of a newly clean junkie, which is what she was, he was sure of it. Just one more white girl with a bad habit trailing her around and maybe, too—who knew—she'd done her time on the streets, going out to Air-line Highway and turning tricks for thirty, forty dollars, more if she blew them, less if she was desperate, who cared just so long as she got her next hit? Had the look: the shuffly walk, the squinty eyes, the raggedy hair, not that he put much mind on her. Mainly she just stayed in her room, anyway. Stayed in there, all curled up in a ball like a baby. Didn't even watch TV. Didn't even turn the lights on. Just stayed in there, in the dark, curled up into a ball like a baby.

Well, he'd seen them come and he'd seen them go, and this one, he predicted, wouldn't last long: wouldn't last more than six months, and then she'd disappear into herself, shrink and shrink until she was no more than skin and bones and then one day there'd be a lit candle in her room, and Miss Lilly would call them all together to tell them that there'd been a death in the family. That's how she put it,

Miss Lilly: Bad news, there's been a death in the family. And the others would all nod and shake their heads, wondering if they'd be next, praying (if they had the sense to pray) that they wouldn't, counting their lucky stars that they were still among the living, even if all they did at Hope House was sit around, watching their T cells disappear and watching TV.

Not that he was complaining: he liked the place just fine. He liked having his own room, all clean and private, all to himself, and no one could come in unless he said they could. He liked the swish, swish sound of Wanda's dust mop in the hall. He liked having hot running water, a toilet that always flushed, and three meals a day, thank you very much, though some of the other residents complained about the food all the time, saying it was bland. He had friends in the place, too. Louis, whose room was right across from his: before he'd taken sick, he'd been a welder. Old Mr. Leon, who laughs at his jokes. Jerome, who can't remember anything, but who likes to talk with him anyway, just passing the time, talking about his old life in Sunshine, way down on the river. Miss Beatrice—she's real nice—coming in every morning, wearing her Baton Rouge Senior Sunshine Team name tag, reminds him a little of his grandmother, all tiny and wizened and sweet. Mr. Jordan a nice man also, wise, always has time to listen. Father Ralph doesn't do much, and never smiles, but Gordon likes him, too. The social workers; the nurses; the cleaning ladies; the volunteers. They were all just fine with him; better than fine. They were caring, decent people, didn't matter if you're black or white, a pimp or a whore or whatever you once were, or if you liked to do it with boys or girls, now you were at the place and they were going to take care of you and that was just fine by him, it was a blessing, yes indeed, it was a state of grace.

Praise Jesus.

They'd picked him up off the side of the road, is what had happened. Literally. That's how low-down he'd become. Picked him up off the side of the road like some dead animal, like road-kill, and hauled him off to Earl K. Long. Pumped out his stomach. Shaved his face. Pumped him up with medicine, with antibiotics, with Norvir and Fortovase and Viracept. Fed him on cherry Jello and Pedialite until his stomach was strong enough and they could switch him to real food.

His sister Ruthie came and said, you're nothing but a junkie but the good Lord done saved you anyway and now you gonna fall down on your knees and thank your Savior Jesus Christ for all he's done for you on this very day. Martha said: I need to tell you now that if you're going to keep killing yourself, if you're going to keep living this way, then I have to say goodbye to you, because I can't just stand here anymore, watching you killing yourself. It isn't natural. I just thank the good Lord that Momma and Daddy have passed on so they don't have to see you like this. His sisters—both of them—were school teachers. They lived in fine brick houses up past the airport, and drove nice clean cars. And every day, it was the same thing: You gonna fall down on your knees and thank your Savior today for saving your sorry butt? Because if you don't, you are lost for good. And on and on they went, hectoring, haranguing, talking at him like he wasn't even there, and then one day, just like that, it happened. A nurse was telling him that he'd gained weight, and was even beginning to look human again, and just like that, boom, Jesus came into his heart. Only it wasn't a boom. It was more like a flash. Yeah, that was it: a flash of brilliant, warm sunshine. Something he could feel in his entire body. *I'm here!*

And Jesus hadn't ever let go, no indeed, not one time since.

But Lucy: he was pretty sure that Lucy didn't know Jesus, and what's more, that she didn't want to know Jesus. Some people were like that. They just couldn't take the Lord's blessings; they weren't ready for Hope House, and it was sad, but it was the way it was. They weren't ready for God's love, and no amount of talking to them helped, either. He knew that for a fact. After all, how many years had people been telling him about Jesus, and yet he'd stayed doing what he had been doing, which was sticking a needle in his veins, stealing money from his own kin, and for what? For drugs. For that next pure high. For a death in the gutter.

Skinny white girl who stayed in her room, curled up on her side, in the fetal position, no bigger than a kid. He figured her to be about thirty, thirty-one, the daughter of some kind of no-count rednecks, the kind that seemed to flourish like cotton in South Louisiana, white and black, it didn't make no difference if your father was a drunk and your mother was a slut, maybe hit the kids, or called them names, and then the father came home and whapped everyone around, or maybe even did it with his own daughter: Yup, he'd heard that that could happen too, more in white families than in black families, the father doing it to his own daughter. Made you sick just to think of it. Made you want to grab a gun and do some killing. Because there was evil in the world and then there was evil, and as down and out as Gordon had been, as much as he'd used people, and done dirty, and lived for the needle, he never did take a life away, or harm an innocent person. Because—and this is where his sisters had him—his parents had taught him right from wrong. From the very beginning, they'd told him to never take anything that you can't give back. His father had sat him down and drilled him, saying: what couldn't you ever give back? Until Gordon had finally figured it out and said: a person's life.

What else?

Their, I don't know, their arm or something like that? Like if you got into a fight. A knife fight or something. And you cut some guy's arm off.

What else?

I don't know. What else, Daddy?

A person's happiness. Don't never let me catch you being cruel, taking a person's happiness from them. Understand, son?

Yes sir.

No, he couldn't blame his parents for what he'd done all by himself. Drugging and drinking and whoring around, scaring his wife and kids off, losing his job, losing everything, his wife taking the kids all the way to Detroit to get away from him, telling him that she'd gone to the judge and he'd lost custody, that was that. Telling him to his face that he couldn't see his own kids, no sir, not now, not ever.

But Lucy, he thought, Lucy probably had been abused as a kid, and then went out and abused herself. She had the look, right down to the rabbity eyes. She had the look of a girl who was trained to be a whore by her own daddy, the look of a girl who couldn't die fast enough.

Which was why he was surprised when her folks finally came to visit, and it turned out that they were just as nice as nice could be. The mother brought cookies; the father looked nervous, pushing his hands deep into his trouser pockets, but saying hello and how-you-do like he was visiting a bank, and not just visiting his junkie-whore daughter and her junkie-whore friends at the AIDS house, which is what Hope House is, when you get right down to it: a place of last resort, for people who'd come to the end of choice. Dressed all nice, the both of them; looking just like any ordinary couple, the kind you'd see at a shopping mall or the movies, the kind that go their own way, mind their own business. Drove in from Lafayette and when Lucy saw them she said, Mom! Daddy! and threw her arms around them. Happened right out front, in the common room, because that's where she'd been, watching TV. Watching *The Price is Right*, because by then she didn't spend all day sleeping, she'd started coming out of her room. The mother passed around the cookies and the father looked at his feet and finally all three of them went outside, out to the little closed-in patio area where there were chairs and a couple of potted plants, pretty plants too—ferns and what-not—and sat and talked. It was summer, hot as blazes. Gordon could see them from inside, could see the way their lips were moving, and how

Lucy sat way up front on her chair, all squinched up to the edge like an excited child, waving her one good arm around.

Hope House wasn't actually all ex-whores and junkies, though at first, when he'd first arrived there, that's what Gordon had thought: he'd thought it was a place for ex-whores and junkies to die in when they didn't have any other place to go. But it wasn't true. They didn't all die, even. Some of them even got better, and left. Louis was his best friend, and he was about as straight-up as you could be, doing welding at the big plants—Exxon, Geismar—that would have been until he got sick. Funny thing, too, that you could have a friend in a place like that, a real friend who you could shoot the breeze with, and tell stories; but there you had it, grace coming upon him like dew on the grass. When Suzette, the volunteer, came, she'd drive them all over in her mini-van, drive them up to the K-Mart on Florida Boulevard for socks and undershirts, things like that, or to the discount CD shop that Gordon knew about off Gus Young, he and Louis laughing like crazy when Suzette fussed at them to put their seat-belts on, or bawled them out about minding their language. It was all in good fun, though: Suzette didn't mean it, she was all right, rich white woman coming in once a week to drive a couple of niggers around, lecturing them to eat right and treat women good. Fellow across the hall, a fellow named Tommy who moved out a month or so after Gordon had moved him, he was a math teacher: went back to work, is what he did. Moved to New Orleans and got a job in the Orleans Parish school district, teaching seventh graders how to find the common denominator, and figure out the y factor when two plus y equals 9. And then there was that white boy, the one whose walls were covered with pictures of half-dressed men, and Miss Lilly fussing at him just about every day to take the pictures down, they were too provocative, they disturbed the other residents, there were rules, and if you can't abide by the rules, well, then, they'd just have to see you to the door. But everyone knew that Miss Lilly wasn't about to kick Alvin (that was the white boy's name) out; Alvin had been living at Hope House for years already; he'd been there longer than any of the other residents, longer than a lot of the care-givers and nurses too; he could practically run the place by himself if he had to, and what's more, he knew things before anyone else did, including who was bringing weed in and smoking it in the bathroom, and who was getting some of what they shouldn't be getting no more, fraternizing within the walls, and who had a wine bottle stashed in his coat pocket, and who was going to die before they even really understood that they were sick. That was another thing: some of them were so young, so young and so low-down, that they didn't even know what they had, which was what he was telling Lucy, the first time, ever, that the two of them ever really sat down and talked. By then she'd put on a couple of pounds and had lost some of her rabbity look, but she still walked with a bad limp, and was too skinny, leaning on her cane, her right arm hanging by her side, all bent up, and useless from the stroke she'd had, which was another thing the virus could do to you: give you a stroke, a storm in your brain, leave you all bent up, unable to walk, or worse, with half your face caved in like a fish, the other half alive and twitching. It's sad, but it's true, he was saying, that some of them come in here—hell, I've seen 'em myself, and that was even before Jesus gave me the strength to walk again and they're no more than babies. Kids. It's sad. Them laying up there in the bed, don't know what's hit 'em. And when you talk to them about the virus, you know, use the word right out, they're in complete denial. Either that or they just too sick to know what's what. They look at you like you're from another planet. Or they start talking about faggots. You know: that only faggots get it, and they're all white. It's sad is what it is. A damn shame.

She'd looked at him then with shy eyes from behind her eyelashes, and he saw, for the first time, that her eyes were blue, and the lashes black and thick. And there was something else about her too, that he hadn't noticed at first, not all those weeks when she was curled up on her side in her room, or even all the weeks since, since she first started coming out to the common room for her meals and to watch TV: there was a certain innocence about her, a certain way she had of holding her head cocked slightly to one side, which made her small chin look like it was pointing somewhere, or perhaps asking a question.

Gaud, she said. That's just gaud-damn awful. He laughed then, hearing the Cajun inflection in her voice.

What's so funny? she said, and he could have sworn she was blushing.

After that, he told her stories. Stories about growing up in Scotlandville, before drugs hit, and how it was back then; stories about the Gold Coast, which was what black folks called the neighborhood right around Southern University, the area where the professors and the administrators lived in proud brick houses surrounded by myrtle trees. Stories about his crew; stories about his wife—or rather, his ex-wife, because he wasn't going to deny it, he had driven her off. Driven her off, her and his two kids too, with his drugs. There wasn't anything he didn't do, either, back then, back before he'd been picked up from the gutter by the hand of the Lord, delivered back to the light of day. Heroin. Marijuana. Cocaine. Crack. Speed. Hell, he was a walking chemistry set.

Never did finish school, neither, he told her. My sisters, they both went on to college, earned their degrees. But me, I was too busy for that. Too busy getting high.

Ain't that the truth, she said.

She was easy to talk to, was what she was. Easy, and she didn't judge him. Unlike the black sisters, who looked at him like he was dog meat, like he was something they'd scrape up off their shoe. Or maybe that was just his wife, before she left him, before she finally got so disgusted that she took all her things and packed up the kids and got in the car and kept driving north until she couldn't drive any farther, driving all the way to Detroit before she finally stopped. Then had a lawyer write him a letter, demanding that he give up custody. Too high to even know what he was signing away. Didn't care. Didn't care about nothing, just so long as he could get his next fix. But Lucy wasn't like that: she'd sit beside him, nodding and laughing, and every now and then she'd give him this sideways kind of glance from underneath her eyelashes, making Gordon feel like he was special, like he was somebody, like maybe there was a reason he was still alive, when so many others were gone, track marks in their arms and the air around them stinking of death.

He told her this story: What finally made me scared? Well, you see, I had my friends, the fellows I called my friends that is, you know how it is, when you're into drugs, you don't really know it, but your friends, the people you call your friends, are really your enemies, because they're the people you're doing drugs with. Let's see: there was Willy, I knew him from all the way back, from when we was kids, coming up. Me and Willy and his brother, Joe, we used to steal the girls' underpants and their brassieres from their mammas' clothing line, parade up and down the street with it on our heads, then we'd run like crazy, you know, when their mothers found out. Got a whipping anyway, but that was the way it was back then. Then there was a fellow named Craig, never did learn his last name. He held up a liquor store, ended up in Angola. Bunch of us, really, all of us in and around Scotlandville, just getting by, though honestly I don't remember it. I couldn't go to sleep in those days thinking that if I had a single dollar on me, I'd get killed for it, but that's just the way it was, living the life.

She nodded, and her hair—which was straight and brown and cut straight across, like a boy's—shimmered, catching the light.

Well, one day, I'll tell you, because this is what happened.

Willy? He was staying at his family home, you know, the same place where he came up. Ain't nobody else living there because the whole neighborhood, it went downhill. All the respectable people, the parents with kids to raise, moved out. Willy's brother, Joe, he moved out too—moved all the way to Texas, if I remember correctly. The whole neighborhood ain't nothing but a place for junkies to shoot up and to get killed. But Willy stayed, because where else did he have to go? Stayed in the family house even after the plumbing and the electric had been turned off, and there wasn't nothing in it but maybe a mattress on the floor and a broken-down TV, because everything else had either been sold or stolen. So anyway, one day, we all kind of look around and realize that we haven't seen Willy for a while. For a week maybe. Go looking around. No one's seen him. No one's heard from him. Go knocking on his door but the place is locked and ain't no one home. A few more days go by, and then I heard what's happened. All the dogs in the neighborhood? All the stray dogs, that the pound doesn't catch? They hanging out in Willy's yard, just standing around, barking, barking like they going crazy. Turns out that that's because Willy's in the kitchen—what used to be the kitchen before he sold all the appliances—dead on the floor, a needle in his hand, cockroaches the size of your fist crawling all over him, and the smell! And that's when I said: I had enough. I don't want no one to find me lying dead with a needle in my arm.

I done some pretty bad stuff, too, Lucy said.

✳ ✳ ✳

She was, he learned, thirty-five years old. Never been married. Had no kids. Spent time on the streets, just like he thought. Started using young—twelve, thirteen—because, she said, she wanted to feel good, wanted to be liked by the popular kids at her school. He had a hard time imagining that, what the popular kids at her school must have been like, because she had grown up in a new subdivision near Lafayette, in a three-bedroom house with air conditioning and a swing-set in the back yard, and she was supposed to have gone to college, too. She was supposed to have followed her big sister to LSU, and gotten a degree, and made her folks proud. But instead she fell in love with the life and ended up on the street, spreading her legs or opening her mouth, and before she knows it, no one's talking to her any more: not her older sister (who became, of all things, a social worker), or her maw-maw, who had cancer only Lucy was too strung out to go see her to say goodbye before she died, or any of her cousins, or her parents. She didn't blame her parents, though: they were Catholic. They went to church and prayed for her soul.

I just about did kill them, is what I did, she said.

They were sitting out back, because by now it was getting to be late fall, and the weather was cooling down some, especially at night, when the shadows fell, and everything got all soft and dreamy. That was the first time he noticed, really noticed, what she looked like. Not like before, when he'd seen her as a compilation of parts: round face, pointy chin, shiny hair, hips as narrow as a boy's, and not much in the way of female softness up top, either, all of that, no doubt, all hollowed out of her, all stripped away from her years on the street. But now, as she reached over to tap her cigarette ash into a glass dish, adding her ash to the heap of ash and butts already in it, he saw how long and delicate her hands were, even the hand that didn't work right anymore; he saw how graceful, and lovely, was her body. She was like some pretty little animal; like a pretty animal you'd see in a forest, the kind that would run away from you, scared. Not that Gordon knew a thing about pretty animals, or really any kind of animal, not to mention forests. Where he'd grown up, they'd had one park, that was it, and it only had a couple of trees, and as for animals: the snakes and the lions and the tigers in the zoo were enough for him, he didn't much care for the animal kingdom, although once he'd had a dog, Barker, whom he'd loved like it was a child. (Whatever had happened to Barker, he wondered, and then realized that he'd lost Barker around the same time that he'd lost Melinda and the kids, all of them gone, all of them as far away from him as was possible in this lifetime, making tracks, putting up a wall of miles.)

She was dressed as she always was, in loose cotton pants and a T-shirt, with flip-flops on her feet. No makeup, of course, because what was the point of putting make-up on when the highlight of your day was taking your morning meds and having the care-givers fuss at you because you weren't drinking your juice at breakfast? (Actually, he thought, that wasn't quite true either. Some of the women— particularly the sisters—put on makeup every day of the week, didn't matter how sick they were, laid up in the bed.)

I don't know, she said, exhaling a thin blue spool of smoke. I just don't know.

That's when he noticed that the insides of her wrists were threaded with spindly blue veins, a whole map of veins just there, just inside her pale white skin.

Did he love her? Sometimes he thought he did. Other times he just thought he was crazy. Crazy, or desperate, or both. He hadn't had a woman for a long time, and that was the plain truth, but now wasn't the time to be correcting that situation, not here, not at Hope House. Plus, right around the same time, a terrible thing happened. It was his friend, Louis. Louis, who he used to ride with, riding around in the car, every Thursday morning when Suzette, the volunteer, came. Riding in Suzette's mini-van, with Louis and sometimes another resident or two, going up to the video store to get Louis a whole bunch of horror videos, weird shit with titles like *Blood Friday* and *Evil Comes at Midnight* and *Satan's Crossing*, because Louis could sit in front of the TV, hour after hour, and watch that shit.

Louis, like Gordon, was a good-looking man, the flesh still on him, his face still shiny and bright. Had had him a life, Louis had, and from the looks of it, was on his way back to that life, back to life on his own, get himself his own apartment, get his job back. He was doing that well. But then—wham—Louis ends up in Earl K. Long, with a runaway fever, and the next thing you know, he's on a respirator.

That's when the volunteer drove him over. Drove him over to see his buddy Louis at Earl K. Long. Drove him and drove one of the caregivers, too, a real nice woman, name of Dianne. Because, the volunteer said, it would be awful not to say goodbye to him, it would be awful not to have a chance to say goodbye to your best friend. Talking the whole time, blah blah blah, about how he had to say goodbye to his friend.

When they got to his ward—ward 5C, intensive care—they were given masks to wear. But Gordon didn't want to go in; no, he truly did not. He didn't want to see Louis like that, all hooked up to machines.

The women went in first, while he waited in the hall.

I just can't, he said when they came back.

He needs you.

I just can't see him like that.

He's unconscious, but he'll know you're there.

By this time, both women were crying: the white volunteer, the one who came like clockwork every Thursday morning, talked too much but otherwise was all right, and how many rich white ladies are willing to hang out with the brothers to begin with? She was crying. Dianne was crying too. Women and their tears. Made him uncomfortable, seeing them crying like that. Made him feel like scratching himself all over, like walking down the long windowless hall, walking and walking and never coming back, no, he did not want to see his buddy all laid out and breathing on a respirator, or watch women cry.

Just for a minute, he said.

He put the mask on and crept in, and at first it was hard

to tell what was going on, whether his friend was alive or already dead, that's how weird it was—his friend's big strong body laid out, as if on a slab, and his rich brown skin, nearly the color of raisins, covered with what looked like powder. His feet sticking out from under the sheet and up top, his big chest covered by no more than one of those throw-away bright blue coverings that they make out of synthetic materials. His eyes half-open but glazed-over, and his chest heaving with the effort, straining against the machines. His hands were upturned on the bed, the palms a whitish-pinkish color that Gordon had never noticed before, and his fingernails had grown long from disuse. He was Louis, but not Louis. He was like a statue of Louis.

I've just got to take the bitter with the sweet, he told Lucy, afterwards, after he had returned from the hospital in the back seat of Suzette's minivan, gone into his room, and had a few private words with Jesus. Just got to take the bitter with the sweet.

I'm sorry Gordon, Lucy said. I really am. And she leaned forward, and with her one good hand, she touched Gordon's knee.

I am too, baby, I am too, he said.

If he was in love, which he still wasn't sure of, it sure didn't feel like anything he'd felt before. Not like with his wife, Melinda. He'd been crazy for Melinda, and that had been the God's honest truth: that woman had made him crazy: crazy with desire, crazy with jealousy, and just plain crazy. First time he laid eyes on her, that was that: he had to have her. Big-boned woman with a generous behind and a quick, big smile, a smile that made her eyes dance, and her hair all teased up into one of those crazy dos like she was trying to be Angela Davis or something, women still wore their hair natural in those days. She'd only been twenty, maybe twenty-one when he met her, and he wasn't much older, but he'd gone after her like she was his own personal treasure, he was a treasure-hunter and she was his gold, and by and by she agreed to marry him, laughing that she must be crazy to marry a crazy colored coon like him. But that had been way back, back when he still had his habit under control, back when he was still driving a truck, making a good living, too, driving those big babies, eighteen-wheelers hauling everything from factory parts to tulip bulbs, driving all over the continental United States, then coming home to Melinda. But no sooner had he walked in the door than it was: Honey, will you see if you can fix the sink? It's all backed up. Or: Praise Jesus you're home I got two sick babies and I feel like I'm coming down with something myself. She changed, too. What was once generous flesh became fat, and what was once a joyful laugh, a kind of crazy pride in how outrageous he could be, became a frown. So yes, he's not proud of it, but he did it: he had other women. It was easy, out on the road. He met them everywhere. At bars. At clubs. Bought them a few drinks and if he got really lucky they'd invite him home with them, and sometimes, too, they came back to his truck, and they made love right there in the sleeping compartment of his cab.

There weren't that many of them, but each time he did it, he knew it was wrong. But he was young, young and stupid and horny and lonesome. Didn't know a good thing when he had it. Didn't know enough to leave things alone.

But with Lucy, things were different. He felt tender towards her, like he wanted to protect her. He wanted to put his big strong arms around her and breathe Jesus right into her mouth, so Jesus would flow down her throat and fill her heart and her lungs and her veins and her bones, so she wouldn't hurt any more. So she'd never cry again. So she could go home to her mother and her daddy in Lafayette, and say: Momma, Daddy, here I am, I've come home.

When the word came down that Louis had died, dying there in his bed at Earl K. Long, surrounded by people who didn't know him, people who didn't know enough to hold his hand or touch his brow, Gordon felt a blow, as if he'd been hit in the guts, as if there weren't enough oxygen in the room. He went to Lucy, to tell her, and she looked at him with big eyes, eyes like a fawn's, and stood there, nodding. But she didn't touch him, or do much of anything other than reach for the pack of cigarettes that she always kept in her right hip pocket, and offer him one. He prayed for guidance, but Jesus didn't answer him, either, and then he had to pray for patience as well as guidance. And then, boom boom boom, things started happening at Hope House, like they sometimes did, real fast. A brother and a sister moved in together: Loretta and Bunny were their names, and when they weren't squawking at each other, they were squabbling with everyone else. Loretta was one of those horse-like women, tall and somehow raw looking, with lips that always looked shiny and puffed-up, like the inside of a plum, and with hair sticking up all over the place, shuffling around in slippers, and what do you know, no sooner than she had moved herself in, gotten herself comfortable, she's coming on to him. Sliding her big-assed self right on up to Gordon and saying and doing all manner of things all leading to the same one thing. Doing it right in front of Lucy, too, saying, You sure are one good-looking nigger, which was not only offensive, but embarrassing, too, talking that way in front of white people. Wiggling her big bottom in his face when he's having his breakfast, sliding her tongue around in her mouth. And the brother, if anything, was even worse, one of those poor souls who you don't even know how to start understanding, with a big head and enormous feet and hands, but what does the man do? He parades around in his sister's clothes—wearing her bright pink fuzzy slippers, her bra and skirt. Then another resident, a black boy who never did do nothing but listen to music on his headset and eat bowl after bowl of Lucky Charms, he wanders off one day and never comes back. His room was taken by a man named Donny, a white man whose arms and chest were covered with tattoos, and who, when Gordon went in to introduce himself, started babbling on about whores and niggers. He was out of his head. Even so, it was downright confusing, and in the meantime, there was Lucy, always Lucy, hovering on the other side of the window, a hair's breadth away, a breath away. Lucy, who came to him now in his dreams, entering him in his sleep like a wind.

It was hot again outside, when he and Lucy smoked, summer coming, and already all the scrub woods around Hope House looked like they were about to catch fire, everything on fire: the houses, the buildings, the billboards, even the pavement of the parking lot. Shimmering with heat, contagious, and day after day, no rain.

One day she told him a story. The two of them were sitting under the awning at the side-door, looking out at the driveway, and there in front of them is the flower garden that some former resident had planted, planted and then died, because that's what happened here: they came here to die, everyone knew it, wasn't no secret. Came here to die because they either didn't have families or because their families didn't want them no more. His own sisters had given up on him which was why he was here, and as for Lucy, her parents had had to turn their backs on her, too, what with her whoring around, her drugs, the men she took in, her stealing, her cheating, her lying. Yup: she'd told him all about it, down to the last ugly little detail. Everything, or at least everything that she could remember, which left some stuff out because she was blacked-out or nodding-off or beat-up or unconscious and in a hospital or bleeding on some mattress somewhere, didn't much matter, she didn't care.

But this story wasn't about those days. This story was about a friend of hers that she'd had when she was young, when she was still just a little thing coming up in her parents' house, before she'd gone bad. This friend, she said—her name was Mary—was closer to her than her own sister was. She was her best friend, and that was a fact, the kind of friend that she did everything with, and told her dreams to. We were pretty much the same size, too, so we could borrow each other's clothes and everything, she said. When we grew up, we were going to go to college together, share an apartment, everything. We were going to be in each other's weddings, and name our children after each other, and live next door for the rest of our lives. That's what we planned. Plus, after college, we were going to join the Peace Corps. We used to talk about it, how we were going to go to Africa, see the lions and elephants. Oh! I just loved those elephants. I probably spent the night at her house a thousand times. And you know what happened?

Gordon shook his head, no.

Ain't nothing happened except that Mary, I don't even know where Mary lives anymore because when she grew up, she left town, left Louisiana even, and every time for I don't know, for ten years, every time I called her house, talked to her mother, her mother wouldn't tell me a damn thing, and then her mother, Mrs. Batiste, starts hanging up on me. Saying, I'm sorry Lucy but I can't talk to you and then, click, she hangs up. Then the phone number gets changed so I can't call there no more anyhow. And Mary? She was beautiful. Just beautiful, I tell you, with these real big old brown eyes and crazy curly hair, and I just loved her. I did. I loved her so much.

You really loved that girl, Gordon said.

I did. I really did, Lucy said, sniffling a little, sniffling into her hands, because all this time, all this time that Lucy had been getting slowly better, slowly beginning to walk right, slowly beginning to put on weight, she had never cried or carried on in any way, leastways not in front of Gordon. But now a terrible thought came to him, and he didn't know why he hadn't thought of it before, that maybe Lucy preferred women, that maybe that's why she'd never opened up to him, not really, or at least not in any womanly way, not even when she'd seen Loretta go at it, switching her big behind back and forth. It was almost as if she were in love with this old girlfriend of hers, this friend from before all the bad things happened, like she could never want no Gordon, not all this time, not with her wanting Mary. Pain blossomed within him then, blossoming inside and spreading out through his veins and capillaries, his nerve fibers, his bones, until finally he was shimmering with it, aglow. He looked at her real long and slow then, looking at her in a way he'd never looked at before, with wide-open eyes, with eyes that begged, taking all of her in, not caring if she was uncomfortable, or self-conscious before his gaze. Taking in every little bit of her, from her small, sharp nose to her wispy straight brown hair, her narrow hips, her slightly pink, slightly freckled skin that stretched down from her neck and plunged under her blouse, encompassing her soft, wet, secret places, and when he saw the blush spreading across her neck and face, he kept looking at her, because he had to, because he had to know who she was.

Will you pray for me, Gordon? she said so softly that at first he wasn't sure she'd spoken.

He took her by the hand then, her small pale hand in his, and right there, right on the patio outside the side door where the care-givers let themselves in, right there overlooking the parking lot and, beyond it, St. Stephen's Home, which was for oldsters, hundreds of them in there just drooling and nodding off in their wheelchairs in the sun, Gordon and Lucy got down on their knees, and began to pray. Jesus, Jesus, Jesus, Gordon prayed—aloud, because Lucy had asked him to—Lord God come into this woman's heart, come and heal my sister Lucy, bring her closer to You, fill her with your love, heal her broken wounds. And on and on he went, praying to the Son, coming to the Father through the Son, praying for Lucy, but praying for himself too, praying until he couldn't hear himself pray anymore, praying until the words were so deep inside of him that they leapt out of his throat before he knew what he was saying, praying without thought of time passing or awareness of his own body, his own breath, his own skin, and when he was done his face was wet with tears and Lucy's eyes were closed and her lips were moving, her hand still in his, and he knew, right then, that Jesus was with him, that He was with the both of them, that Lucy, too, was a child of God, that she had been redeemed. And that's when he married her—because that's just what he was going to do, marry her and make her his wife—because he knew that Jesus was with both of them, working through them and in them, forever.

Praise God, he said.

Praise God, she whispered by his side.

YOU DON'T KNOW NOTHING ABOUT ANYTHING

Every few months, a new volunteer would come. At first
—at the old house downtown—the place had been crawling
with volunteers, mainly pampered women of that peculiarly
Southern variety of pampered that varied in its particulars
from place to place but was basically the same package everywhere: a former sorority sister, now married to a doctor (or
lawyer, or investment strategist, or real-estate developer), with
children old enough to be in school, and time on her hands.
Typically, she'd be a member of the Junior League as well—or
if not the Junior League...except that it always was the Junior
League. They tended also to be blonde, though hair color,
obviously, wasn't as much a defining feature of this set of
women as attitude and life-style. But back in those days—
when Hope House was crawling with volunteers—it was also
crawling with fairies. Now Hope House is chocolate city and
Alvin's the sole remaining fairy in the joint, not to mention
something of a survivor, having been condemned to die two
or three years back. Of course, they still have the Senior Volunteers, Miss Beatrice and Mr. Jordan, except that Mr. Jordan
had had to abandon his job as a retired volunteer and go back

to work with the lettuce at Albertson's.

And anyway, Alvin's explaining to the most recent new volunteer: "It was sort of chic back then, to have your own personal fairy to take out to lunch or go shopping with. But once all the fairies, with the exception of yours truly, died, all the Junior League ladies went away. And now we just have you and Miss Beatrice and Father Ralph."

"Who's Father Ralph?"

"You haven't met him? He comes by every couple of weeks. He's been doing it for years. He doesn't talk much."

They're driving—or rather, she's driving, because she's the one with the car, whereas he's the one with the almost-non-existent T cells—to do errands: to the Albertson's, where Alvin wants to get ingredients to make a cake for Miss Lilly's upcoming birthday. Actually, it's going to be a birthday torte: a caramel-almond torte with spiced mango compote, to be exact. He'd only made it once before, and that had been years ago, when he and Edward were still to-gether, living in that lovely little house in the Garden District like the two perfectly-matched fairy queens that they were. Well, they *were* fairy queens—there was no denying it. With Alvin fussing over recipes and obsessing about extra-virgin olive oil, and Edward with his own flower business, they were such a cliché that Alvin was constantly surprised when Hollywood didn't come calling, wanting to do a knock-off of their lives, calling the show something like, "The Boys of Baton Rouge," or "Louisiana Loves Lyle and Lou," (Lyle and Lou being, in his imagination, the names of the sit-com characters based on Ed and himself.) How he'd slaved over that torte, his brow getting all red, the sweat pouring down his ribs despite the air-conditioning. He even remembers the dish he'd made it in, a heavy, old-fashioned canary-yellow torte dish that he'd picked up at a junk store somewhere way down on the bayou, Napoleonville perhaps, on one of their treasure-hunting trips. Not that there were so many of those, either, given how busy they both were—Alvin with his catering business and Junior Leaguers, Ed with the flowers. Really, it's amazing he even remembered about that torte, given everything. But he wants to do something nice for Miss Lilly's birthday, and God knows that none of the other residents will bother to do anything. In fact, no one's even supposed to know that she so much as has a birthday: Alvin had found out by accident, because he overheard her talking on the phone, probably to that bastard of a husband of hers, the one who was always running around with other women, only Miss Lilly didn't even know it, and if she does, she's in denial, unable or unwilling to read the signals, which to Alvin were as obvious, and as glaring, as a red-light flashing on top of an ambulance. Oh well—his heart goes out to her, and that's the truth. Menopausal, married to a jerk, and on top of everything else she's not aging well, not with that white-white skin of hers and delicate, upturned nose. Such, however, is the way of blondes: for a few years they're spectacular, and then, with few exceptions, they fade.

"I know I'm almost fifty," is what she'd said. "What's your point? And no, I do not intend to do anything on my birthday, I just want to forget about the whole thing. What do you want me to do? Plastic surgery? You know what?

You're not as pretty as you once were, either."

Sugar, ginger, oranges, lemon, cinnamon sticks, mangoes, almonds, potato starch....or maybe he should make his famous double-chocolate-chocolate pie, and top it with fresh strawberries. Only no: that wouldn't be a good idea. Too many diabetics in the place, including himself. Also, he'd have to get the strawberries on the morning of and God knows that the chances of getting good fresh strawberries on any given day aren't necessarily so great, not to mention that he'd need a lift to and from the store, and even if he did call a taxi, who could guarantee that the taxi would show up on time? There was the savory option too: crudités, wrapped shrimp-balls, cheese platter. But no, that too was a no-starter, not with this crowd, and not for a birthday. Because a birthday, especially a big birthday, deserved something special, something that you can't buy at a bakery or even order at a good restaurant. Something good enough for the gods.

"So what does he do when he comes?"

"Who?"

"Father Ralph?"

"I don't know. He prays, I guess," Alvin says, blinking rapidly behind his thick glasses. And that's another thing that has gone downhill, way downhill, since his diagnoses: his eyesight. But at least, thank God, he hasn't gone blind, like that poor crazy sweet old Jerome, or, for that matter, Mr. Leon. "Plus he has this thing for Miss Lilly."

"He does?"

"Oh God, yes. Like for forever already."

"How do you know?"

"Honey, everyone knows."

And after the Albertson's he wants to go to the Dollar Store for toiletries, and then he has to get to his storage unit, so he can retrieve his Cuisinart, if he can find it in there with all his other stuff, with his baseball cap collection and tuxedo and cookbooks, his furnishings and rugs and television set and lamps and decorations, because once upon a time he'd loved to decorate for Thanksgiving and St. Patrick's and just about any other holiday that came along, why, he'd just swathe the house with tinsel and bulbs and all manner of tacky banners, which drove Ed, who was a purist, crazy. Like the time he'd attached red roses—the fake kind made of silk—to the ceiling of their bedroom: when they lay on their backs in bed they gazed up at a field of red blooms. Or the time that he and Ed threw a party for the entire block, inviting all the little old Southern widows and the Republican yuppie couples and all their kids besides, and served chicken-and-shrimp shish kabob over saffron rice with a warmed herbed salad, and hung Mardi Gras beads from all the branches of the trees, such that their back yard glimmered and danced with light. Because as Alvin had always maintained, if you're going to be a fairy you may as well go all the way. Hell, when a Jewish family moved in next door, he even threw a Hanukkah party, making potato latkes (with a recipe from *Gourmet*) and buying draydls for all the children, and a Jewish prayer-beanie with the words "Chappy Cholidays" in bright red letters sewn onto it by himself. Which reminds him. He could use some new clothes. If Suzette is willing he really wouldn't mind going to the Burlington Coat Factory, too, just to look around, because, as everyone knows, the Burlington Coat Factory doesn't just have coats, and in fact doesn't even primarily have coats, but rather, has all manner of clothing, not to mention bric-a-brac and candlesticks and throw rugs and home décor items, and now and then he finds something there that he just has to buy, if not for himself, then as a present—for his mother or one of his nieces or even one of his fellow residents at Hope House, because let's face it, most of them were utterly destitute, and when their SSI checks came, they went out right away and spent it all on crawfish po-boys and cigarettes. So it's up to him. Only, truthfully, because he's not feeling all that great today, he doesn't know how much longer his energy will hold up.

"What was it like growing up in Texas?" Suzette now asks, interrupting his reverie. She's a nervous driver, hitting the breaks long before she has to, and tapping them as she approaches red lights, which drives him nuts. But she's pleasant enough, and not stupid. Why she's doing this he can't quite fathom unless she's one of those people who's fascinated by death, and hovers around, hoping to catch a glimpse of it for herself. Angels of Death is what Jay, who for a year or two was his roommate in the old house, used to call them: women who got into death and dying, who went to all the funerals, and appeared to love nothing better than delivering eulogies. But Jay: he'd died alone in the hospital, which was exactly how he hadn't wanted to die.

"Or would you rather not talk about it?"

"What?"

"Texas."

"In Texas, when I was coming up, if you were gay they'd first try to shame you out of it, and then try to preach you out of it, and if neither of those worked, they'd haul you off to some Christian therapist who'd pick your brain and talk Jesus to you until you were so confused that all you could do was weep."

"Tell me about it," Suzette says.

"Honey," Alvin says, "You don't know nothing about anything until you grow up gay in Texas."

He can play up the gay thing, or he can play it down, depending. Like when they finally got to the Dollar Store, and the woman behind the cash register was giving the two of them the eye, as if maybe Alvin was going to spray all his gay genes all over her, instantly transforming her into a dyke? He played it down; in fact, he even let it be assumed that he and Suzette were together, which they certainly weren't, and wouldn't be even if Alvin was straight, given that Suzette isn't his type at all. No, because in general he preferred the chirpy, cheerful Junior Leaguers of his yesteryear, because even if they weren't particularly interesting, at least they stayed with the script: oh Alvin. How are you today? Feeling all right? Where do you want to go to lunch? There's this absolutely darling café that just opened up near Catfish town. Want to try it? And by the way. My hair color? Do you think they put in too many highlights? Should I go back and have it toned down? Whereas he got the feeling that Suzette actually wanted to have a conversation. With the Junior League set, on the other hand, it was all gossip and small-talk, decorating and

parties, easy and comfortable, with no one afraid that someone might slip up and actually say something. Moreover, such
prattle played to his strengths: after all, for years he'd been in
the catering business, making large quantities of shrimp *étoufée*
and pecan-crusted salmon and chicken-with-mushroom-wine-
reduction for the fund-raisers and coming-out parties and
birthday celebrations of Baton Rouge's moneyed classes. It
was a funny thing, too, because as poor as Baton Rouge was,
with miles and miles of decrepit shot-gun houses and empty
lots and black teenagers hanging out on street corners working on their careers as future convicts, there was plenty of
dough in Baton Rouge, too. Plenty. Which he hadn't believed
at first—when he'd first arrived out of Texas A & M to take a
job with Sears, of all places—but saw soon enough. There
was the regular doctor-and-lawyer-and-engineer money, which
could get you pretty far in a town like Baton Rouge where the
housing wasn't so expensive and there were no taxes to speak
of anyway, and then there was the real-estate-development
and oil money, which could buy you a mansion in the Country Club of Louisiana plus a camp on some bayou somewhere, not to mention skiing vacations in Colorado and
shopping trips to Houston. And it was that crowd—the
Country Club of Louisiana crowd—who had made his little
catering business, Creative Cuisine, so successful.

*Oh Alvin! Your sauce piquant is just divine! And how on earth do
you manage to get such good tomatoes at this time of year?*

He was a full-breed fag by then, too, not like some of the
men he'd met, even at Hope House, who, if you didn't know
they were gay, you'd never know. The fact of the matter was

that being gay was good for business. Which is something he'd try to explain to his old roommate, Jay, more than once, but Jay was one of those old-fashioned gentlemanly repressed homosexuals who went out of their way to dress like good ole boys, in khakis and loafers. He hadn't even told his own family that he preferred men until he was almost forty, and even then he hadn't actually said the word "homosexual," but rather, had confined himself to vague hints and euphemisms until at last they'd caught on. Alvin suspected that Jay's parents must have been morons. What, Alvin had wanted to know, did Jay tell them when he moved into Hope House? Because there was no getting around the fact that the only people in Hope House were people dying of AIDS, and that, back then, every single one of them had gotten the virus from doing it with guys. Not just with guys, but up the asshole with guys, and in their mouths, and any other way they could do it, or have it done to them. Well, humans are no more and no less bestial than animals themselves are: shitting, fucking, sucking, killing, eating, farting, belching, barfing, masticating, masturbating, and then starting all over again. And yet! There was more to life, after all, then getting it on—as Alvin of all people knew. Because Alvin, unlike almost everyone he'd ever known, and that would include heterosexuals too, had known True Love.

His own parents had taken the news of his orientation in their stride, probably because they'd seen it coming for so long. Either that, or because his brother had tipped them off. Either way, they didn't cry, or yell, or threaten him with being kicked out of the family, or anything else other than wince. And at least he'd left home, where he could go and live his life somewhere far away, where they didn't have to see him prancing around his house in December, festooning the Christmas tree with ornaments of copulating men or Santa Claus with a hard-on. They knew about Ed, too, but, thank God, didn't insist on spending more than a minimum amount of time with the two of them. But Jay? Poor Jay had been so ashamed, right up until the very end, that he'd ended up dying alone.

Alvin's mother and father call him almost every day. They want to know how he's doing. They want to know if he's ready to move home yet. But as he always says: That's sweet of y'all, but what the hell would I do in Beaumont?

Amazingly, he'd been able to locate not just his Cuisinart, but also his favorite cookbook, meaning that he won't have to reconstruct the torte recipe from memory. Because really: he wants the party for Miss Lilly to be nice. And while he's at it, he'd gone ahead and bought party hats and party favors too, because what kind of party is it if you can't make funny noises and look like an idiot doing it? And in the meantime, there are his usual duties which primarily involve gossiping with Annie and Dianne, and sitting with a young resident named Yolanda, listening to her bitch and moan. He also sits with Veronica, who is totally and one hundred percent out of it, but nonetheless doesn't seem to be in any hurry to die, and he used to sit with Jerome, too, but that was when Jerome still had enough brain cells to formulate a sentence. But these days he mainly sits with Yolanda, because even though he can't say he feels any real affection for her, his heart goes out to her anyway. Poor thing: she'd only moved in around the time that Suzette had started volunteering, but already Yolanda had managed to alienate just about everyone on staff, and half the residents too. Suzette, for one, can't stand her, and Alvin knows that for a fact, because Suzette had told him so. Miss Lilly is up in arms about her, too, complaining that she accuses her of stealing her money, and won't bathe. Even Annie, whom he adores, as in adores, is frustrated by her, complaining that no matter how loving she is towards her, Yolanda throws her love back in her face, saying only that Annie's not her mother, so she doesn't have to do what Annie says. Of course, if she'd had a mother to begin with, she probably wouldn't have ended up at Hope House, but chances were that, like with so many of the young girls coming in these days, her mother had been a womb only, and then did little more than see to it that Yolanda didn't actually starve to death. You saw them like that, just driving around or going to the Walmart or the grocery store: young dazed mothers screaming at their kids, or hauling off and slapping them, or worse, which always made Alvin suspect that if they were this negligent in public, they were probably ten times worse in the privacy of their cramped and nasty little homes. Plus Yolanda's a homely little thing, her arms and legs covered with sores and no bigger than twigs, a set of buck teeth that stick out so far they're practically horizontal, and swollen feet, and she's getting sicker every day. Even so, the girl is vain, fussing with

what's left of her hair, primping in front of the mirror, looking at the fashion magazines that Alvin provides for her,
and, when she feels up to it, spraying herself with cheap,
overly-sweet, nausea-inducing perfume. Which he is so not
in the mood for, given that his own stomach is so jumpy
that it's not even funny. Thank God that today she merely
smells somewhat stale: the result, no doubt, of lying around
in the bed forever and a day.

"So," he's telling her, "I thought and thought and
thought about if I wanted to make maybe a pure chocolate
torte, but then I realized I needed to find something festive,
but not so sweet that it will send half our residents to the
emergency room."

"Uh huh," Yolanda says, which for Yolanda is a lot.

Yolanda lies with the covers pulled up under her chin.
Even so, he can see the sharp, bony protrusions of her elbows and knees. Funny how some people blow up and others, himself included, shrivel away until they look like con-
centration camp inmates.

"You eating enough?"

She nods her head, yes.

"Me? I just can't keep any weight on. Not that that's necessarily such a bad thing. I used to be kind of heavy."

"You mean fat?"

"Not to put too fine a point on it, but yes. I was fat. My
whole family is fat. Plus. Did I ever tell you that I was in the
catering business? A professional liability, I suppose, because
before I served anything, I had to taste it. Suffice it to say
that I did a lot of tasting. But now—" and he gestures with

his palms turned to the ceiling "—as you can see, I'm not exactly a heavy-weight."

"How much you weigh?"

"One hundred and thirty or so."

"I weight one hundred two."

"How much did you used to weigh?"

"Dunno. Lot more."

"Well anyway, at least you've got your appetite, and that's the important thing. Not that you don't get tired of the food they give you here. I mean: scrambled eggs and grits. Scrambled eggs and grits. Scrambled eggs and grits. How many scrambled eggs and grits can you eat?"

"I like my eggs fried. With bacon. Don't like the way they do it here. It too dry."

"I couldn't agree with you more."

"And I keep askin Dianne to get me better eggs and she jes keep saying she gon try but morning come and it look like nasty dried out eggs again."

"Well, she's not in charge of the food."

"Then why she say she gon help?"

"Probably because she means to."

"And Annie! Bossin me around all the time, like she think I's a retard."

"I just love my Annie bird," they can hear from the hall, as Veronica, strapped into her extra-large wheelchair, goes by.

"What wrong with that fat girl?" Yolanda continues. "Talking stupid all the time."

"She's sick. Just like you. She can't help it."

"She stupid, though. Annie bird. More like a rat. Nasty

rat, into everyone's business."

"She's just trying to help you. Annie can be a little brusque, but inside, she's a pussy cat."

"Shit."

And he sits there for a little while, gazing out the window, until he hears the *Oprah* theme song floating in from the sitting room out front, and decides to join whoever might be watching.

For the torte: Preheat oven to 375°F. Blend 1 3/4 cups almonds, 2 tablespoons sugar, potato starch, and cinnamon in processor until nuts are finely chopped, about 45 seconds. Using electric mixer—I forgot my electric mixer! Or wait: do I still have one? Or did I give it away? I supposed I could do it by hand but it will take forever—beat egg yolks, 2 tablespoons sugar, and almond extract in large bowl until very thick and pale in color, about 3 minutes. Fold almond mixture into yolk mixture. Using clean dry beaters, beat egg whites, and salt in medium bowl until soft peaks form. Gradually add remaining 4 tablespoons sugar, beating until stiff but not dry. Fold large spoonful of whites into yolk mixture to lighten. Fold in remaining whites in 2 additions. Transfer batter to 9-inch-diameter springform pan. (Shit! Where'd I put my springform pans?) Bake torte until puffed and golden brown and tester inserted into center comes out clean, about 30 minutes. Immediately invert pan onto rack. Cool torte (upside down) completely.

"You sure you know what you're doing?" It's Suzette, standing somewhere behind him, as he crawls up into his storage unit.

"I know they're in here somewhere."

"You know, it might be easier just to go to the Walmart and buy new."

"Yes, except that the junk they have at Walmart is cheap cheap. Doesn't hold up well at all."

"How much cooking do you plan on doing?"

"Just give me another minute. I'll find it. I'm sure it's all in here somewhere."

Really, he doesn't need this aggravation. Because first of all, he doesn't exactly feel full of vim and vigor to begin with, to say the least. In fact, he's full of aches, like maybe he's coming down with the flu. Second of all, he had to wait an entire week for Suzette to come back so she could drive him to his storage unit, and then he had to wait another hour or so while she ran an errand for Veronica, and on top of everything else another new resident moved in, who unfortunately is white. Unfortunately because the guy thinks that because Alvin, too, is white, the two of them are meant to be friends. Which, as far as Alvin is concerned, is never going to happen. Because, just for starters, Donny is covered in the most appalling tattoos. Also, he's plain old nasty, with stringy hair, and God alone knows what kinds of homophobic and racist and who-knows-what kinds of hateful attitudes and assumptions. Because the thing about living at Hope House is: you don't have to love it, and you certainly don't have to love the food, but you have to get along with everyone, and if you don't, well, that's just your tough luck, because eventually, if you push it enough, Dianne and Annie will get on you, and then Miss Lilly will throw you out. And then you'll be back on the streets, where you started. In fact Alvin is the only current resident living at Hope House by choice. Not that the others were forced, or anything like that: but for them, it represented an alternative to life on the street. Whereas Alvin could have moved home to his parents in Beaumont years ago, and even now they're happy to have him. Or at least that's what they say: Alvin, you know that your old room is ready for you any time.

Just what he needs: living at home, with Mom and Dad, his high school yearbooks, and all that green shag carpeting.

It's just that when he tested positive, things started sliding downhill fast, not just with his health, but, really, his whole life. The only person who knows the whole story is Annie, and he'd only told her because one night, a few years ago, he spiked a fever and thought he was going to die. But the truth is that in the end, Ed had been anything but loyal. The one who he considered to be his True Love, and whose company was so delightful that, when he was with him, he felt that he'd entered a state of bliss—of magic, of happiness, of light and laughter and charm—had abandoned him, utterly, to his illness. The one he'd pictured growing old with; the one who called him Honey Bugs and Wabbit, and other silly pet names, and who swore that the two of them had been lovers in a former life. Ed was a handsome man, too, with water-blue eyes and a broad, strong back that curved seductively during the height of love. But in the end he was nothing but a slut, and worse, a coward. (Which is how he knew what a giant scum-bag Miss Lilly's husband is—because once you've lived through it yourself, you can read the signs as clearly as if they were electronic billboards.) Only Ed's still walking around in the world, making flower arrangements for debutante weddings, and infecting God knows how many other innocent men, whereas he, Alvin, the infectee, is dying.

"I bet that hurt a lot," is what Annie had said, after hearing the whole sorry saga. Hurt? It still hurts. It will never stop hurting. There's a hole where my heart used to be. Not to mention the shame, because even though he was the wronged party, he felt that he was wearing a sign that said, "Ugly Fat Homo Who Isn't Even Good In Bed Which Is Why My Boyfriend Ed the Magnificent Has Found Something Better."

"Here it is!" he now announces, pulling an entire nest of springform pans from a box perched on top of the other dozen or so boxes crammed into his storage unit.

"Jesus, Mary, and Joseph, a miracle has occurred."

"Just wait until you taste my torte, if you want to see a miracle," Alvin says, but then he remembers that he still has to locate his mix-master.

He likes TV as much as anyone but really, how many times can you see the same rerun of *I Love Lucy*? But at least he tries: there's the garden, which sometimes he putters in, pulling up weeds and watering, and there are the occasional occasions—someone's birthday, or the Fourth of July, or Thanksgiving—when he can get his decorations out and make the place look festive. And he makes himself useful, also, by helping the other residents, especially when they're new. Which is why it's such a drag for him when Donny starts yammering away, talking all kinds of nonsense, and insinuating that the two of them have to stick together. Stick together with a racist redneck homophobic asshole? He doesn't think so.

And anyway, not that he's told anyone, even Annie or Dianne, about it: but he really hasn't been feeling well. He's used to not feeling well, of course, but this time it's different, because the pain, when it comes, comes as if from his deepest being, as if what was inside his bones was not marrow but the virus itself. He could picture the virus, a million-million minuscule monsters, like piranhas, equipped with over-large, viciously-sharp teeth, swimming in a sea of fetid goop. And that's what his insides are: a sea of fetid goop, slowly being eroded, literally eaten away, by an alien life-form. They fed on him, those piranhas, making a meal of his liver, his kidneys, his heart, his bones. They infested his sexual organs, swimming into his gonads and down his urinary tract and to the very tip of his penis. They fed off his skin and the back-sides of his eyeballs. He was like a dog with worms; or a malarial African.

✳ ✳ ✳

For the compote: Combine sugar, mangoes, water, potato starch, and egg whites in heavy medium saucepan. Bring syrup to boil over medium high heat, stirring until sugar dissolves. Boil syrup 5 minutes. Pour into medium bowl; cool 30 minutes. Mix in mangoes. Cover and chill at least 2 hours and up to 4 days.

It will be wonderful! Because not only is he going to surprise Miss Lilly with a beautiful torte, but also, he plans to have flowers, and streamers, and he's organized everyone so that when she comes in the morning they'll be waiting for her, wearing silly hats and yelling "Surprise!" By now just about everyone's in on it, too, because when you make a party—even a surprise party—you need the cooperation of the people you live with. Annie and Dianne are helping with decorations; Miss Beatrice has promised to pick up some cold drinks; and even Donny, of all people, has promised to help, though whether or not he can do anything is anyone's guess.

He dreams that he and Suzette are driving to church, only when they get there, it's not a church at all, but a swimming pool, and Father Ralph is standing there, in a little black bikini, with a whistle around his neck, and Alvin can't help but notice the outline of Father Ralph's penis under the slick black material of his swimsuit. For a moment he feels lust but then he sees that there are snakes in the swimming pool, and worms that curl around each other. Father Ralph blows on his whistle, but now he's standing there stark naked, only where his penis is supposed to be is a large, bloody hole. And then it becomes apparent that Alvin has to get in the pool and swim laps, because if he doesn't, something terrible is going to happen. He protests, but Suzette just shrugs and says: what's the big deal?

But by now he's angry, and he yells back: the big deal is that you left me! You were supposed to love me and instead you left me!

I never loved you.

When he wakes he's sitting on the sofa, next to Yolanda, who's dressed in a shiny green running suit, with big furry pink slippers on her feet, and watching a rerun of *Dallas* on TV.

"You awake?" she says.

He's seen them come and he's seen them go, and most of all, he's seen them die. Sometimes, in fact, he's the last one to see them alive, or even, on one or two occasions, the one who's been with them when they take their last breath. Unfortunately, he wasn't with Jay when Jay died, because Jay was carted off to the hospital, where he died alone, without a single soul to comfort him, to hold his hand, too stroke his beautiful cold forehead, to whisper that he was going to God or that he was loved. Poor Jay! Sometimes Alvin even dreams of Jay, and in the dreams he is always trying to convince him to leave the store (what store?) and come out to the lake (what lake?) to take a swim, and every time Jay refuses to leave, and then Alvin begs and wheedles but still Jay won't budge and Alvin wakes up on the verge of tears. But he's seen plenty of other people out from this world to the next, and every time, it's the same: one minute there is life, and the next minute, there's this thing in the bed, this object that used to go by the name of Mary or Toby or Jerome or Jancine. And then what? Ah! The million dollar question!

He wonders about it too, because it isn't like he never studied history, and was unaware that, even before AIDS, whole scads of people have died before him. Only somehow all those people who died in all those wars never really impressed him as being as fully human as he is, but perhaps that's only because he'd never met them. All those wars, from the dawn of history onward, not to mention starvation in Africa and tsunamis in Asia, child-prostitution in India and the Holocaust, Pol-Pot, Stalin, hurricanes, famines. As a child, learning for the first time about the horrors of life in the Olden Days, when people dropped like flies from everything from the flu to starvation, he simply assumed that his own life's trajectory would be nothing like that, that he—like all six of the Brady Bunch kids—would grow up in a clean and pleasant house with clean and pleasant parents and go on to have a clean and pleasant life until he was so old that he didn't really count anyway, so it wasn't any real loss, even to himself, when he died. Who is he, though, to have expected such things? The cards he'd been dealt told another story, and his own little life, as important as it is to him, apparently means next to nothing to whoever it is who rules the universe.

A week or so before Lilly's party, he wakes up dreaming that he's in a public toilet with feces and urine and soggy, soiled paper streaming up backwards out of the bowls, and though he's desperate to relieve himself, he knows that he can't, not here, and not with so many other people lined up to use the facilities. But what's this? His eyes are open now, blinking in the dark, and he realizes that the excruciating pressure in his bladder and along his spine is real, and that he's in his room at Hope House. There on the windowsill are his favorite stuffed animals—Bear, Pussy, Sweetie-Pie, Laurence of Arabia—and there across from the foot of the bed is the shelf with his prized statue of an erect penis (a gag gift from himself to himself that he'd bought one day in the French Quarter) and his books, family photographs, and his collection of plastic dinosaurs, which can only mean one thing: that the bathroom door is just over there, on the other side of the room. He gets up, finds his slippers beneath his bed, and begins to pad towards the door, when the pain in his lower back runs down his legs, his bladder all but explodes, and he falls with a crash to the floor. Well, shit almighty, he thinks. If these are my death throes, I'd really rather not be here. Right before he loses consciousness, he feels hands on his shoulders, and hears a woman's voice calling his name.

He comes to in a hospital room, with a broken hip, and a leg in traction. His personal belongings—toothbrush, hairbrush, dental floss—are in a plastic container on the nightstand, and someone's brought him two sets of his own pajamas, his slippers, and a bathrobe, and taped a poster of a bare-chested George Clooney on one of the walls, but otherwise the room is decorated in High Institution: gray tile, stained acoustic tiling; icky-yellow blanket. On his second

46

day, Annie comes to visit, and sits holding his hand, like she does, and preaching at him to thank God that he lives in a place where they got medicine to help him, where instead of being left in his own filth to die like a dog he was taken to the hospital to feel better. "Count your blessings," she says: "You here, you loved, we all cares about you, and you still got breath in yo' body." She sits next to his bed, her big, warm, strong hand enveloping his, as if she could pass her vitality on to him through her palms and fingertips. He gazes at her, his eyes enormous behind thick lenses, his cheeks sunken, and his pale white skin blotchy and discolored, and knows that she is as good and as kind as anything he's ever known. Even so, and even though he knows she's right, he doesn't feel particularly lucky, let alone blessed. He feels alone and frightened and depressed. There will be no getting better for him, no triumphant return to Hope House, no war stories about the time he busted his hip like a little old lady, no therapists fussing over him to take just one more step, that's it, Alvin, you're getting stronger by the day. How does he know it? He just does. Worse, Miss Lilly's surprise party will never happen, nor will he ever make that fabulous apricot-almond torte, or see her face when they all burst into the "Happy Birthday" song. And somehow that's the most depressing thing of all, because really, the party for Miss Lilly was going to be his swan-song, his last burst of creative magnificence, his last attempt to do what he'd been put on earth to do. When he cooked, it wasn't even as if he, personally, were doing anything extraordinary, but rather, simply allowing what was supposed to happen, happen.

Brown sugar. Almond extract. And then the lovely surprise, the relaxed and peaceful feeling people get when they bite into something so delicious that it recalls the sweetness of summer, the look of surprised happiness that comes upon adults when they're allowed to be who they really are, which is, as far as Alvin is concerned, children. But now every part of his body hurts, and he can't imagine doing so much as lifting a spatula. Doctors and nurses come, take his vital signs (that's a good one, he thinks), examine his hip, talk about infection and bed sores and eventual physical therapy, and urge him to keep the fluids going. "For a moment we thought you wanted to leave us, cowboy," one of the doctors, a young man with bright red hair and pudgy fingers says, "but then we got that infection under control, and now it looks like you gonna be with us for a while."

But the days drag on, and other than his brother, who drives down from Memphis for the day but whom he doesn't much like, and Annie, who comes by when she can, no one comes to visit. (Miss Lilly calls daily, but what with all the trouble with her asshole husband, and all the trouble with her dying charges—well God knows she has enough on her hands.) All those women whose parties he'd organized, all those gay-men's balls and holidays and celebrations, only to come to a non-existence that was even worse than death, because at least when you were dead people couldn't come to visit you, and you wouldn't have any use for them even if they did, whereas now he has to lie in his own tomb while still conscious, breathing, and having to go to the bathroom. His parents call every day, but he's told them not to come, not yet anyway. "Mainly I'm just bored," he says. "Don't worry, I'm not dead yet." They cry and tell him that they can't stand the idea of his being alone in a hospital, but he assures them that he's fine, and that anyway, he's not alone, not with all the doctors and nurses coming by every two minutes. "Frankly," he tells them, "I'd rather see you when I'm back on my feet." But he doesn't believe a word that comes out of his own mouth, and is always surprised when his parents concede to his wishes. Because (and despite Annie's visits and Miss Lilly's phone calls) he is alone, and he's soon to die. At night, Jay visits him in his dreams, his face a ghastly white and his arms and legs missing, and sometimes he's crying, and sometimes he's begging, but always he strikes Alvin not as friend, but a freak, a warning, a hallucination, and Alvin wakes drenched in sweat, only to blink through the darkness, and the liquid electric light coming in through the room's one window, until he finally remembers where he is, and how he got here. One day he calls Miss Lilly on the phone and says: "Please don't let me die here! That's all I ask! Don't let me die here!" and Miss Lilly says: "Alvin, we're going to take you home just as soon as the doctors get that hip stabilized."

But he's not so sure, and he's even more not so sure when Father Ralph shows up one day, his white collar smudged, his big stomach flopping over the top of his pants, his black hair brushed sideways over his bald spot. "So," he says, entering the room in that soft-heeled way employed by members of the clergy when they don't want to scare you, "I understand you took a tumble."

"Something like that."

Father Ralph pulls up a chair, and sitting heavily, the silver cross around his neck bouncing off his protruding stomach, he leans forward and, after a prolonged silence, during which it seems to Alvin that Father Ralph is fighting sleep, says: "Anything I can do for you, while you're here?"

"Thanks, Father Ralph, but I'm good."

"You don't look so good."

"I look like pure hell, if you'll pardon the expression. But no. Annie comes to see me, you know, and Miss Lilly calls, and they feed me here and everything. I wouldn't mind some decent food, but you know how it is: I can only eat soft food, things that are easy to digest. It's all rather gruesome, actually."

Pulling something from the inside pocket of his jacket, Father Ralph says, "Can you eat candy?" There's a Hershey's bar in his hand.

"Candy? I don't think so. What with my diabetes."

"Oh," Father Ralph says before leaning back in his chair, folding his arms over his chest, and falling silent.

Fuck! He thinks. If Father Ralph is visiting I really must be bad. They're all lying to me! Even Annie! I am so on my way out.

Once again he dozes off, dreaming of Jay, and his mother, and groups of naked men copulating in small dark places, and he thinks: why can't I join them? He tries to will his dream-self into the huddle of naked copulating men, feeling the pressure in his lower regions, the blood running to his prick, the pulsing need to move his hips, to hump, to find a pair of buttocks to rub against—and maybe if I'm horny, he thinks in the dream, I'm not dead—when a commotion interrupts his dream and penetrates past his unconsciousness to wake him into a dark afternoon. Standing before his bed are several people. Or maybe they're not people. Maybe he's dead, and they're heavenly beings. Only he knows he doesn't have that kind of luck. He wonders where his glasses are.

"Quiet now, y'all, can't y'all see he's sleeping?"

"So what we came all this way to see him don't you think we oughta wake him up?"

"He don't look so good."

"Of course he don't look so good, fool, he dun broke his hip."

"Well I don't care I gon go wake him up. Goddamn."

"Hush up, alls of you. Let me or Annie wake him up real gentle-like. No need to give the man a heart attack."

"Quiet, everyone! We in a hospital, not a nightclub."

Blinking, Alvin reaches for his glasses. "Hey," he says.

"Surprise!" they say together, and now he sees that not only have they all come—Gordon in a new blue track suit, Mr. Leon in a wheelchair, Annie and Dianne in their uniforms, Lucy looking like the little slut she is, Miss Louise with some greasy shit worked through her hair, Miss Lilly looking pleased and scared at the same time, and even Suzette, who, as usual, looks out of place and uncomfortable—and even, and this is unbelievable, the repulsive racist homophobic redneck Donny—just about everyone, in fact, but Jerome and Yolanda, but also, they're all wearing paper hats, and holding small shiny metallic-looking objects in their hands. Here in the hospital, they look even homelier, sicker, and more pathetic than usual, as if the earth had coughed up the dregs and sent them straight to his room, just to get them off the streets.

"How'd y'all get up here?"

Suzette raises her hand.

"And y'all fit into her van?"

"You should have seen us!" Donny says. He's wearing a grimy black Grateful Dead T-shirt and basketball shorts from which his skinny scarred-up hairy white legs stick out like two blanched carrots. "The way this chick drives, holy shit! Lucky we didn't get into no accidents because the cops, man, they would have hauled our nuts straight into jail, all of us packed in there like sardines, and in the middle of the whole thing Mr. Leon decides he can't wait to get to the bathroom…"

"Hush your mouth, boy."

"Well, anyway, we here."

He stares, amazed, when Annie explains: "You know, we knew you was feeling poorly, and getting down on yourself, down on your whole life."

"That right," Dianne says.

"So we gets our heads together, alls of us, and we thinking, you know how you was planning on making that nice surprise party for Miss Lilly?"

"You sho' was," Dianne says.

"So we gets our heads together and decide that here you are, and you always doin' nice things for everyone else. So we be thinking: why don't we do something nice for you?

Seeing that Alvin always helping everyone else, we gon see if maybe it our turn."

"Really, you don't have to—"

"We not having to do nothing. See? And we even done bring you a cake."

"But it's not my birthday. My birthday isn't until June."

"Don't matter. This have nothing to do with birthday. This have to do with: we love yous."

A moment later, Donny—who had been huddling at the back of the small crowd and then slipped out of the room entirely—appears again, and approaches Alvin's bed, holding what appears to be—what is it, anyway? Because the misshapen blob that Donny presents to him on a plastic platter is anything but a cake. Perhaps it's a dish of oatmeal? But no, on closer inspection he sees slivered almonds, brown sugar, and apricots. "I found your recipe, dude," Donny says. "Only I think maybe I totally fucked it up!"

"Don't worry about it," Alvin says, but really. He's supposed to eat this?

"And another thing, dude," Donny continues. "Is that Miss Louise, she made you another cake, so you got a choice."

And now Miss Louise, her black jelled curls shining under the sickly fluorescent lighting, strides forward, the large object in her hands—a sheet cake? a slab of shit?—blazing with candles. At the same time, someone shuts off the lights, and together they sing the birthday song, only instead of saying "happy birthday," they sing "happy because-you're-here day," or at least that's what he thinks they say, it's hard to tell, because while Annie sings loudly, her beautiful resonant voice coming from deep within her soul, the rest of them apparently can't sing worth a damn, which is weird given that most of them are black, and, in his experience, black folks, more often than not, sing like angels.

"Thank you," he says.

But they're not finished. When the song is over, they start marching around his bed, blowing on kazoos, which makes his head hurt even more than it was hurting before. At last, the performance over, Miss Louise places the cake, or whatever it is, on the bed where his left leg would be if his left leg weren't still dangling in a cast from a Medieval-looking contraption attached to the ceiling. He sees bananas, lots of white frosting, and his name, in blue sugar.

"What is it?" he finally asks.

"You never had banana pudding?" Miss Louise asks.

"Banana pudding?"

"It's got the bananas, see, and the bottom layer is those Nilla wafers, and in between vanilla pudding, you can make it instant if you don't have a lot of time, and really it better that way anyhow, but for you, because you diabetic and all, we got the sugar-free type of Jello pudding, tastes just as good if you ask my opinion, and the Nilla wafers they hardly have any sugar in them anyway, mainly corn syrup, and Miss Lilly say you can probably have some, no problem about that, ain't that right Miss Lilly?"

"That's right," Miss Lilly says, glancing at her watch.

Which begs the question: does he have to eat this mess? This foul concoction of every ersatz food-stuff ever dreamt up in the bowels of hell? This confusion of chemical flavorings and toxic preservatives? Perhaps he can get away with swallowing a single piece of sliced banana, claiming that he has no appetite?

"Here baby," Miss Louise says. "Seeing that it your day. You get the first piece."

Shifting himself up onto his elbows to accept the offering, Alvin says a silent little prayer: Dear God, don't let me vomit. But when he finally lifts the plastic spoon to his mouth, what he tastes is cool lemony sweetness, like a wish.

JEROME AND THE ANGEL

Jerome had two secrets, both of them so beautiful that he wanted to burst open, just burst right open at the seams, spilling himself everywhere, all over the floor, all over the ceiling, filling the whole room up like the sky, filling it and filling it until there was no Jerome anymore, and no room, either, but just one big Jerome-room, walls, floor, table, dresser, comb and hair sheen on the dresser, all the same thing, all of them shouting glory hallelujah, praised be God.

The first secret was this: Jerome had an angel, his own personal angel who visited him regularly, coming through the window at all hours of the day and night, whenever he felt like it, because that's what angels do: they come whether you're expecting them or not, or even if you believe in them, which Jerome didn't at first. Even after he'd seen him with his own two eyes, he didn't believe in angels, and the angel had had to come back again and again for Jerome to finally believe in it, for Jerome to finally know what he knew. But the thing was that his angel, at the same time that he was Jerome's angel, was also Jerome: he and the angel were both separate and merged, the both at the same time, only it was kind of hard to explain. He didn't much want to explain, anyhow, seeing as the angel was a secret. Not that the angel had told him to keep quiet. The angel didn't much care one way or another if other people knew about him. It was more Jerome's idea, because Jerome liked the idea of having a secret, particularly here at Hope House where everyone was into everyone else's business, they couldn't much help it, all of them living side-by-side like they did, and taking their meals together, and nothing to do all day but sit around and talk, sit around and watch the TV, sit around and eat, and sit around and talk some more, because there just wasn't anything to do, and even if there had been, it wasn't like he could just go out and shoot a few hoops with the fellas, not with his legs not working right, and his eyesight all but gone, and his hands all heavy, and everyone waiting on him to die. That was the hardest part, the part that even after the angel started coming to visit him, he couldn't much face, and didn't want to think of: how he had come to this place to die, how they'd put him here—his sister, his mamma, the doctor at the hospital where he finally went after he'd had that first stroke, when he was just minding his own business and there was a storm in his head and down he goes and the next thing he knew he was up at Earl K. Long, tubes stuck in his veins, in that room he'd never seen before, and a sign up over his bed that said: Jerome Johnson, HIV POS. Meaning that the doctors and nurses and everyone, all the people coming and going there were so many of them that he couldn't keep track, they had to wear special gloves and special masks because they didn't want to touch no Jerome, couldn't handle him too closely, especially not his blood, no, because his blood was where the culprit lay, his blood was infected, filled with tiny uncannily intelligent creatures, like fish with scorpion's eyes, like something from the bottom of the deep sea, only so tiny that you couldn't even see them under a microscope, and those creatures—and the doctor who finally sat on the side of the bed to explain it to him said so himself—were responsible for what had happened to him when he'd suffered his collapse, back there in where is it you say you're from? Sunshine? Back in Sunshine.

They'd put him here to die. Thirty-four damn years old and they'd trundled him up like an old potato and put him here to die. Didn't make any damn sense at all, how someone his age could just up and die like that, his body turning on him, all invisible inside his skin, but that's why they'd put him here, after all. So he wouldn't die alone and raving out of his mind like Grace had, screaming about devils and Satan and what-not, all crazy-eyed and skinny, pus pouring out of the sores in her skin, pus filming over her eyes, spit and saliva everywhere and his pretty little Gracie—his Grace, his good-time girl, knew how to love him up and loved him up good and plenty—she's dead and buried in the ground, gone to Jesus, and there ain't a damn thing he can do about it.

You go try lying here up in the bed day and night just day and night I be lying up in the bed ain't not like it used to be and I got me a pain so bad in my side but I gon get better I'm taking my medicine every day I take them and just as soon as I get my strength back, just as soon as I get the strength in my legs back, I be moving back home, going back to Sunshine, I'm going to get my old job back, you ever been to Sunshine, Miss Beatrice?

Well now, sweetheart, I can't say I have.

Even when the angel first started coming to see him, taking him by surprise, Jerome didn't say a damn thing about him. Not a word. He talked about everything else: about home, and Grace, only she died, and their little boy, Jerome Junior. Jerome Junior was living with Jerome's sister Yvette, being raised up right, but never would know his mamma or his daddy, though once or twice or maybe it was more than that, because Jerome never could much remember, his sister Yvette had brought the little boy in, held him on her hip over Jerome's bed, saying: that's your daddy, boy. Don't you want to say hello to your daddy? A little boy with his mother's enormous brown eyes and his father's wide, square head. How you feeling today, Jerome? You looking like you doing okay.

Yeah, well.

And sometimes she brought clothes and sometimes she brought shampoo and batteries and things like that, things she thought he might need, even though he didn't really need much of anything, not the way he was, lying up in the bed like that, all day long, his legs long and heavy and useless below his waist, just lying there like two sacks of grain, filled with all kind of shit and not working right, they wouldn't hold him if he tried to stand, wouldn't much do anything but just lie there, part of him but not really: part of who he used to be. Only that was a dream too: who he used to be. A dream that he'd sometimes think was only a dream from start to last, a dream within a dream that he'd had one day when he was lying up in the bed, like he does every day. The volunteer brought him things too: skin cream, a chocolate bar, a Bible. Sat next to his bed reading from the Bible only she was white and pronounced her words as if she were chopping them off with her teeth, it wasn't that she didn't know how to read good, it was just that she didn't know how to get right into it, reading the word of the Lord the way it was meant to be read. But it wasn't her fault, being white and all. The very first time that the angel came he told him exactly that. He said: ain't her fault she don't know how to read good. She doin' the best she can and you can't right ask her to do no more than that. And Jerome had just had to sit back and agree, because—and this was the point—there wasn't much use in arguing with an angel.

That first time he came to visit, he just walked on through the window, all regal and grand, like maybe he was some kind of celebrity, a movie star going to the Oscars. He'd seen that show, once, but it was a long time ago: all those skinny white movie stars in slinky dresses, showing their titties off if they had them, which most of them didn't. Most of them skinny as boys, with hip bones that stuck out and bottoms with nothing to hold onto at all, no meat, no motion, no nothing. He didn't know a thing about it, not a thing about these white movie stars, couldn't much see what the big deal was all about, the way one and then the other clutched at that little gold statue and started to cry, thank you thank you, thank you so much, oh oh oh!

His angel was so beautiful that at first he couldn't do anything but stare. He could see him as clear as day, too, even though most of the time he couldn't see nothing and no-body, just shadows, swirls of colors, outlines, blurs. Miss Lilly would come in and hover over his bed like she did, wringing her hands together and trying to be cheerful, telling him that yes, Jerome, we're going to get you some glasses, I've put a call in to Medicare to see if we can't get them to pay for your prescription, but the glasses never did come, and in the meantime the world shrunk and shrunk until he couldn't see much of anything anymore, not even his room, not even the TV or the window or the closet where his sister Yvette had put the new clothes she'd bought for him at the Walmart, comfortable track suits, the kind he liked, with that nice new-smelling fresh smell. But presto! That angel just comes sauntering in through the window, like it was the easiest thing in the world, like it happened every day, no big deal, ain't you never seen an angel before? Comes on in like that in his golden robes and all that white light shining off him, and just like that Jerome can see again.

Hey, he said.

Who you?

Don't jive me, baby. You know who I is.

You my granddaddy?

Do I look like your granddaddy?

How would I know? My granddaddy done passed before I even born. Mamma used to talk about him all the time, is how I know about him.

No, baby, I ain't your granddaddy. Try again.

Jerome closed his eyes. He felt like hiding. He felt like pulling the blanket up over his head. But he didn't. And when he opened his eyes again, the angel was still there, only now he was sitting down. He was sitting in the chair in the corner next to the bed.

You my angel? Jerome said.

Now you got it, the angel said.

What you want from me? Am I dead?

No, you ain't dead. Do you feel like you dead?

Nope.

Well, you ain't.

Then the angel got very big—he got very very big—filling up the whole room with a kind of sparkly radiance, like he was made of glitter, lots of glittery light, and then, in a whoosh, he was gone again. And Jerome didn't tell a damn soul about him, not even Miss Beatrice, who sat with him nearly every day, or Annie who came to feed him and was always quoting the Bible at him and telling him to put his trust in Jesus.

That was his first secret.

The other secret was: Jerome loved the cleaning lady, Wanda. It was that simple. He loved her with all his heart, loved her from the first moment he set eyes on her, which was way back when, when he first came to Hope House, when he could still see good, before he needed glasses, before he could only see shadows and light and shade and dark, blotches and patches of color, swirls of nothing where outlines and solid shape used to be. Now he loves the sound of her, the wet sucking sounds of her mop in the hall, her deep-throated laugh, and he loves the smell of her too: the smell of cleaning fluids combined with warm skin combined with some kind of baby oil.

Hey, Wanda!

What you want?

When you gon go out with me?

Where you gonna take me?

I take you out to get you the biggest juiciest steak in Louisiana. How about that?

I better go get me a new dress, then. Something pretty.

You pretty no matter what.

She was, too, but not in the way his sister Yvette was pretty, with her kind round face and soft shoulders, or the way Grace was pretty. No doubt about it, his Gracie had been something else, all swishing her behind up and down the street, wearing those tight shorts, driving him crazy, but that had been before she'd gotten sick, when she was still young, still driving all the boys crazy. Would have married her too, married her in a big church wedding but she went and got pregnant with his baby and didn't want to walk down the aisle with her stomach sticking out, said that they could wait until after the baby came, but then, one, two, three, before you know it, she was nothing but skin and bones, big eyes sticking out of her head, arms like sticks, and throwing up all the time, because that's what the virus does to you, you gave it to me Jerome Johnson. You some kind of faggot only you don't tell me? You doing it with guys?

I ain't never gone near no man and you know it. Ain't love no one but you.

Doctor told me that you get it from bodily fluids, Jerome, that means sex, which means I get it from you. Who else give it to me? Santa Claus?

I swear Grace.

You swear what?

I swear, he said again, because what else was there to say? He wasn't no homo, never had been, that was just plain ridiculous. And once he'd hooked up with Grace, that had been it: she'd been the only one for him, he weren't interested in no other woman. Only he didn't say that. He didn't say anything. He done gone and killed her, is what she was telling him, and there wasn't anything to say to that, and anyway, she didn't last much longer after that, a week or two only, the whole time lying in the bed at her mother's house on Peach Street, in the big bed in the front room because that's where her mother, who was sickly herself, who had some problem with her legs and couldn't move real good, could take care of her best. Little Jerome Junior went to Yvette and Grace lay up in the bed moaning and groaning and when Jerome went to visit her after work or on the weekends she'd look at him and yell: you did this to me! You nothing but a murderer! Faggot! Get out of here before I call the police, you the Devil come to get me, Satan! Mamma! Satan! Satan eating me, Mamma, he eating my stomach get him off me! I'm gonna call the cops! Only he knew that that was impossible, too, that Grace didn't have the strength to get up to use the phone, and that half the time the phone was turned off anyhow, because Miss Mary, who was Grace's mother, didn't always pay the phone company on time, not with her other worries, and her legs that didn't work quite right, giving her shooting pains down in her shins, shooting pains like needles going into her shin bone.

Wanda was pretty in an old-fashioned, old-timey kind of way, almost like she reminded him of his grandmother or someone like that, only of course Wanda wasn't anything like his grandmother at all. His grandmother had had sharp long fingers and all kinds of frizzy gray hair, whereas Wanda was soft and round and dimpled, as shiny as newly-laid tar, her hair patted down smooth on her crown, and smooth and quiet with her push broom and her mop, her hips broad and her behind soft, the way he liked women to be.

Hey Wanda!

What you want, Jerome?

When you gon go out with me?

When you gon ask me?

I asking you now.

All right then. Just let me finish up what I got to do here.

You do that, Wanda. But don't forget!

I ain't forgetting nothing, baby.

He could hear her out there, in the hall, swish-swishing her push broom along, and then the smells—her own warm smell of smooth skin and soap and sweat, but not a lot of sweat because they kept it pretty cold inside, the air-conditioners going full-blast against the summer heat, and also the smell of Lysol, of disinfectant extra-strength Ajax, of toilet cleaner.

Wanda!

I coming, Jerome. I really is.

But she didn't come. He waited and waited, but still no Wanda. Instead, Annie came. She came and said: What you know good, baby?

Where's Wanda?

She gone home for the day.

She coming back tomorrow?

He wondered if maybe he was fooling himself, if maybe Wanda had no intention at all of stopping by to see him, but then the angel popped up, saying: Why don't you do something nice for that girl?

Huh? What girl?

That girl you so sweet on.

Other people came to visit him too, other than Wanda and his sister and Miss Lilly and the white girl and Annie and the angel. There was Miss Beatrice, who came just about every day, because that was her job, she was retired but now she came to Hope House every day, it sure beats sitting around at home and worrying myself sick over my daughter—my poor daughter? I tell you about her? Cancer. She's gon be taking her journey soon. I goes to see her every day, but I can't stay there all the time, not without getting in the way, and at my age it's time to give a little something back, praise Jesus. And that priest, Father Ralph, you could tell he was white by the sound of his voice, sometimes he visited too, but he didn't do much talking, just read a prayer or two in his quiet white voice. The other person who came once a day was his nurse, his new nurse because something happened to his old nurse, either that or they'd sent someone else, he couldn't right remember what Miss Lilly had told him, all he knew was that his new nurse came every day, usually in the morning, to bathe him, bathing him right there in the bed because he couldn't get up any more, telling him about where she was from, which was Canada, a special part of Canada that he couldn't remember the name of, is where she was from, way up North, so far North that it wasn't even America any more, it was Canada. He couldn't remember her name but he could remember that she was from Canada. She said: where I grew up, every winter it snowed so much the snow covered the cars and came half-way up the walls of the houses and sometimes covered the windows on the lower floors too, that's how much snow there was, snowing day and night, the whole world white with snow. Not like now. Now it hardly snows at all. And she'd hum and whistle, picking up one limb and then the next, rubbing the damp wash-cloth along his legs and arms, even over his private area but there wasn't nothing sexual about it but even so it made him uncomfortable, the way she wiped him down there, like his penis was no bigger, no more potent than a baby's, but at least she did it fast, going down there in a hurry and then lingering over other places, over his neck and face, his hands, his feet. He couldn't much see her and didn't even know what she looked like and that's because she was a new nurse, she'd started coming after he'd lost his eyesight, all he knew was that she was white. Had to be, the way she talked, drawing out her vowels, flattening them like they were pancakes spreading on the griddle, plus who other than white folks live where there's all that snow? Jerome didn't know much about snow, and that was a fact. In Sunshine, when he was coming up, it had snowed precisely once, and that had been on a Christmas day when he was maybe ten years old. Woke up early expecting to find a tape-recorder waiting for him under the little silver metallic tree that his mother took out once a year, saying she didn't want no big old pine tree in her house, no sir she didn't want to have to go picking up pine needles in her own damn house and anyway only rich people is fool enough to pay good money for a dead tree that they only going to go and throw out. Tape recorders were expensive but his friend Roger up the street had one and he wanted one with all his heart, wanted one that he could sing into, pretending like maybe he was on the radio, the next new thing, ladies and gentlemen this next act that I'm going to introduce comes all the way from Sunshine, Louisiana, let's hear it for Jerome Johnson, the J.J. Kid we call him, put your hands together, folks, let's give him a nice warm New York City welcome.

Oh yeah.

But instead of a tape-recorder there had been a brand-new Bible, picture of the baby Jesus on it, right there on the corner, and a red sweater wrapped in green paper, and instead of sunshine in Sunshine, that day there had been snow. It snowed on and off, little chunks of wet white snow coming down all day long until in the back yard the Iron Plants were speckled with it, and kids went out in the street, trying to make snow men. But the snow was too wet, and in any event, by the next day it was warm again and everything melted and people went around saying: what did you think of our white Christmas? Which was kind of a joke among black people, saying white Christmas like that, because even though no one he knew paid much mind to white folks one way or the other, just kept to themselves and kept out of trouble, the way you're supposed to, everyone knew that it would be a cold day in hell before white people gave black folks anything much more than the time of day.

But this nurse of his, the one from Canada where it snowed all the time, snowed and snowed like the end of the world, like a giant refrigerator, like Alaska and the North Pole all wrapped up into one, she was white, and she bathed him every day like he was her own kin, bathed him and fussed over him and said things like, Jerome, hon, how long you been here now?

Gordon visited him, too. He was a new resident, but he wasn't like the others, talking like they didn't know anything about anything and never would and never wanted to. Gordon had been around. He'd had him a life, with kids and a wife, and his wife had been a good woman, only he'd driven her off, but before he had, she'd wait at home for him every damn day of the week, just waiting for him to come home so she could give him some of her good home cooking, some of that étouffée that she made so good, some gumbo and you like gumbo Jerome? How you like it, hot or not so spicy because me? I like it hot-hot. Came and sat in the bed and talked to him about Jesus. Talked to him about Jesus like he personally knew Jesus, like Jesus maybe was his brother or his uncle or someone. Miss Lilly rubbing her hands together. Suzette who was the volunteer saying: you want me to read something to you? What do you want to hear? Do

69

you have any favorites? And sometimes saying: What, Jerome? Say it again, I'm having a hard time hearing you today. And Wanda, of course. There was always Wanda.

He was going to marry Wanda is what he was going to do. Have himself the big church wedding that he'd wanted to have with Grace—a wedding with a big old party afterwards, with fried chicken and corn on the cob and sweet potatoes and mashed potatoes and plenty of gravy because that's what makes it all so good, but nothing fancy, he didn't want a fancy party, never did like people putting on too many airs. No, his wedding would be solemn but not fancy or stuck-up, and afterwards, why, people would just have themselves a good old time.

Put yourself in Jesus' hands, Annie said.

Put your trust in Jesus.

But what happened was: well, it was so bad he didn't even want to talk about it. He put the blanket over his head and refused to talk. Refused to eat, even. Why should he eat after what they done done to him? Oh Lord, they're trying to kill him!

It wasn't right what they done to him, neither, slipping him into the operating room like that in the middle of the night, and taking all his bones out. Taking every last bone out of his body, so that he didn't have any more bones, so that he was just a sack of flesh, of blood and sinew, of skin, and maybe some other things too, the things you have to have or you die, but still it wasn't right. Do you see the scar where they took my bones out? Right here, right on my side, do you see it? Do you?

I don't see nothing, Jerome. It was his angel again, come to see him after a very long time, because frankly, after the wedding, Jerome hadn't wanted to see much of anyone, not if he could have his Wanda all to himself, and those other guys were just going to have to sit back and be jealous, because she had chosen him after all, saying: now Jerome, you know I love you best, don't you?

His angel was wearing a suit and tie, which was very un-angel like, Jerome thought. Usually he wore robes, like in the Bible. Big, white, flowing robes, and sometimes they were white, and sometimes they had little stripes in them, and sometimes they were more golden, but always it was robes. Not today. Today his angel was wearing a conservative dark-gray suit with a red tie and black leather shoes. Looked like he was all dressed up to go see his lawyer. Either that, or like he was maybe going into the mortuary business.

What you want?

Hey. You the one called me. What you want?

Where my wife?

Your wife is fine. Everything's fine. Calm down.

Why I be calm when you come to take me to the grave?

Why you say that?

Just look at you, man. You look like you a damn undertaker.

The angel glanced down at himself, then went over to the small mirror above Jerome's dresser to take a good long look. When he turned around again, he said, I think I look pretty good.

Well, I like you better the way you used to come. In your God-clothes. The way you all slicked up now, I barely recognize you.

What you going to do now, Jerome?

Huh? What you mean?

You getting ready?

He had to think about that then, thinking about what that meant, to be ready.

I just got married. I'm going on my honeymoon. I just got to finish packing, and then I'll be ready.

Where you going? the angel said.

Florida.

Well, the angel said. Congratulations.

It was Easter. That's what they all said. They said: It's Easter, Jerome, what you think the Easter Bunny going to go get for you for Easter? But he had plans of his own. He had plans, and he had the money too, and the next time Suzette came he told her to just go on into his drawer, the drawer right there next to the bed, just go on in there and get out his wallet where he keeps his money, and just go take that money, and go buy the biggest prettiest Easter rabbit you can find, hear? Because I need a big pretty one. Pink. Big and pretty and pink, and you just go get the best one you can find. And an hour later, or maybe it was two hours, he didn't know, all he knew was that Suzette was standing over the bed—she was the volunteer, and she came in every week, came in and read to him in her funny white voice, deep like a man's—and she said:

Jerome! Jerome! Look! I got you your bunny rabbit. Can you see it?

Oh! It was beautiful. It was big and pink with sticking-up ears, just like he wanted it, and in its little paws was a big old Easter egg, all wrapped in shiny foil. He couldn't see it with his eyes, but he knew anyway. He knew in that new way he had of knowing, from inside his eyelids.

Can you see it?

Yes indeed. Go get her. Go get Wanda. Wanda! Wanda! Where's Wanda!

What you want, Jerome!

I got something for you!

Oh yeah! What you got for me Jerome?

No! I mean it! Come see what I get for you!

Oh Jerome! It's beautiful. Look at that.

It's for you.

He's beautiful.

Want to know what his name is?

What?

His name Glory Glory Hallelujah.

Yes indeed.

He's flying. Flying with the angels. And he can see so clearly it's as if his eyes had become magnifying glasses. He can see the whole world, and he can also see all the people in it. He can see houses and trees, and squirrels and leaves and TV sets and pillow cases and lamps. It's so beautiful, his heart can barely contain it.

Come see! Come see!, he says, and his voice has expanded too, expanded and melted at the same time, so it flows out of his throat like honey. My darling, my darling sweet Wanda, my lover, my wife, my life, my darling sweet thing, my beauty, I love you, I love you, don't ever leave, I consecrate my life unto you, I give you my heart, my soul, I am coming, my darling, don't ever forsake me! Gracie! Gracie! Wanda! Mamma! My angels! My angels! My angels!

Yeah baby, I here. What you want, baby? What can I be doing for you?

But he doesn't want her to do anything for him; rather, he wants to do something for her. He wants to introduce her to his angel. His beautiful, gorgeous, perfect angel, dressed all in blue in shimmery blue in golden blue he's so big and so beautiful all light just like you my darling girl just like you like you like you.

THE MAJORETTE

The thing about Suzette was she wasn't cut out for Hope House at all, and half the time, as she drove up, she was queasy with anticipation, her stomach leaping into her throat and giving her bad breath and sour insides. She didn't really want to go today, either. Just for starters, she barely understood the first thing that most of the people at Hope House were saying, and that included Mr. Leon, who was her favorite, and most of the staff, none of whom, as far as she could tell, had more than a high school education, and probably had gone to schools that barely qualified to begin with. But she'd had to find something to do with herself once the youngest of her children started school, and going back to work full-time was not an option, if only because she'd been out of the game for such a long time. That, and she doesn't really want to go back to work full-time, or even part-time, anyway. She was a lawyer, but she'd found the practice of law to be no more elevating, or interesting, than peeling potatoes. In the law firm where she'd been employed as an associate—with promises dangled before her almost daily concerning her bright future—mainly what she'd done was handled a bunch of greedy small-fry corporate clients who wanted to screw some other greedy small-fry business or bend federal regulations or dump their toxic waste in black peoples' neighborhoods or into some old man's fishing hole, and by the time she'd figured out that she needed a change and started thinking about going to work as a civil rights lawyer or for Legal Aid, she was pregnant. She preferred staying home with her babies, anyhow, holding their warm sweet-smelling skin against her own, comforting them when they were fussy, nuzzling their bellies, and walking them through the neighborhood under the wide deep shade of the Live Oaks. She hadn't much minded getting up with them in the middle of the night, or the way her breasts swelled with milk, or any of the rest of it, either, and had always wondered what her friends were talking about when they complained of boredom, or said that they felt trapped. Two boys and two girls is what she'd had, producing one after the other in even, two-year intervals, delivering each of them with the casual ease of an Olympic ice skater gliding onto the ice.

She was free now, more or less, to do what she chooses —or at least free until three o'clock, when her kids came home from school.   Mainly she wanted to be left alone. Maybe she should get a dog. A rescue dog. Then she and the dog could take long walks together, and when the kids got old enough to not want to talk to her anymore, the dog would still love her. She didn't want to turn into one of those rich, bored women who play lots of tennis and meet their girlfriends for lunch, women who go around with perfectly manicured nails and perfectly coiffed hair, because that's all they do to begin with—go to the hair salon and the nail salon and the shopping mall, with occasional stops at the grocery store or their kids' school, like the mothers of most of her kids' friends, none of whom she has even a shred of a desire to befriend, even though Adam keeps pointing out that every single one of them is really a very nice woman, and that she, Suzette, would be happier if she got over her own sense of herself as being smarter than them. But she can't, and that's because, first off, she is smarter, and second off, as far as she can tell, not a one of the mothers whom she's met through her kids has anything to say about anything whatsoever. An entire generation of well-tended white women who live in well-tended brick houses in charm-less, soulless subdivisions with names like "Highland Estates," and "The Mill at White Oak." Her own mother had been like that, a real Southern belle, right down to the loopy, dumb-sounding accent and the puffed-up black hair—hair the color of black patent leather which only got blacker, and more perfectly lustrous, with time—the blue eyes outlined with heavy mascara, and the matching shoes and pocketbooks. To top it all off, to tie the ribbon at the top of the already pretty package, Suzette's mother had "landed," (the term she still uses,) Suzette's father, a surgeon. Her mother drank too much; her father, the surgeon, had a heart attack and died when Suzette was in college, probably because Suzette's mother was an insane bitch. Suzette had two younger sisters but she was the only one who came out even half-way all right.

Her mother was backwoods Mississippi—which was about as backwoods as you can be and not be retarded and cross-eyed, having sex with your own twin brother while the hound is looking—and the Southern belle bit was all a sham. How Suzette's father had stood her was a mystery, unless, as Suzette assumed, her mother had been spectacularly good in bed. That, plus she'd been gorgeous exactly the way men of her father's generation had liked their gorgeous, with curves, and small white teeth. When Suzette was a girl, her mother had spent a lot of time sipping bourbon with one or another of her girlfriends at the country club, coming home in time to greet Suzette and her sisters when they got home from school. She'd forced Suzette to attend Cotillion, where the girls had to wear white gloves and the boys got hard-ons, and forbade her from reading Richard Wright, Maya Angelou, or, weirdly, Emily Dickenson. Naturally, she'd thrown a fit when Suzette decided to go to law school, only coming around when someone pointed out to her that the law school at LSU was crawling with boys from what she insisted on calling "good families," which was bullshit, as most of Suzette's fellow classmates in law school were middle class kids from nowhere towns who wanted no more out of law school than a way to make a decent living. And she'd only gone to LSU, which she'd attended briefly as an undergraduate and loathed, because she could pay for it herself, thereby avoiding any scenario wherein she'd have to go crawling to her mother, begging for money. It nearly killed Suzette when, during her first year, she fell in love with a third-year student and shortly thereafter agreed to marry

78

him, particularly as she'd had no intention of marrying anyone any time soon, or at least not until she was thirty. Her
mother was delighted. At the wedding (which thank God
Suzette had insisted would be small, without flower girls or
bridesmaids or any of that other shit that she detested), her
mother toasted the bridal couple by saying, "Now you know,
y'all, that my little Suzette the Majorette sure has been givin'
me some trouble over the years, and I don't need to mention
every las' lil bit of it, because you know about my Suzette,
headstrong like her daddy was, always needin' to be doin'
things her own way." She was tipsy. "But today you are looking at a happy mother of the bride, because it was just like
Suzette's daddy always used to say: 'you give her enough
time, she'll work things out for herself just fine.'" She was
wearing very high heels, and a swishy, silky pink dress with a
plunging neckline and jagged hemline, like the serrated edge
of a bread knife. She looked like an aging madam, but even
Suzette had to admit that her mother was well-preserved,
practically radiating with flirty, flickering sex.

"My little Suzette," her mother said. "My married majorette."

"Suzette the Majorette." She hated that, her mother's
nickname for her. In school, her friends, picking up on her
embarrassment, called her "Suzette the Teacher's Pet." By
junior high this had evolved to "Suzette the Space Cadet,"
coupled, once Suzette stated her belief in the equality of
women, with "Suzette the Suffragette." After her first semester at LSU, she was called "Suzette the Flagellate," which
was stupid, because not only had she never raised her hand
or any other object at her disposal to inflict pain on anyone

whatsoever, but also didn't even rhyme. No matter. "Flagel-late" became "Fellate," which was equally stupid, and also didn't rhyme, which then became "Suzette who's always wet," which did in fact rhyme, but made equally little sense. Eventually, she'd graduated summa cum laude, with a double major in philosophy and English, but by then she'd trans-ferred to Wellesley, where she read all of Shakespeare, and studied modern dance.

Hope House, she thinks, is about getting back at all that—not just at her mother and her mother's ludicrous, narcissistic, antiquated, selfish, stupid and fucked-up-the-butt expectations for her, but her own history, her own sullen, stained sense of who she was. Her therapist (who constitutes yet another ex-pense, on top of the four children, that Adam worries about) seems to think that, even if she is getting back at her mother by purposefully hanging around with junkies and prostitutes, Hope House is a good idea for her. He folds his hands together on his lap and says: "Whether or not you consider yourself a religious person, or even believe in God, what you do at Hope House is a both a form of therapy, for yourself as well as for the people there, and a form of wor-ship." He himself is a practicing Episcopalian, a concept which Suzette finds vaguely hilarious. On his walls are ab-stracts composed of a lot of cream colors—cream brown, cream white, cream yellow—punctuated with a slash of bright blue or a splotch of orange. The art, she thinks, had probably been chosen by his wife.

She liked her therapist anyway, and had told him all kinds of things about herself, focusing on her mother, the death of her father, and her husband, Adam, who lately, and for reasons that she couldn't figure out, seemed to be turning into exactly the kind of husband whom her mother had wished for her: steady, hard-working, high-earning, and somewhat dull, with breath that smells of the mint toothpaste he favors, and a closet-full of Dockers. What she hadn't told her therapist about was just about everything else. For example, she hadn't told him about the real reason she goes to Hope House every Tuesday and Thursday morning, rain or shine, which has almost nothing to do with getting back at her laughably transparent mother and everything to do with how she'd gotten her hideous college nicknames. She hadn't told him that no matter how squeaky clean and conservative she was in her personal life (had she not done the entire stay-at-home-mommy bit?) she still feels like a teenage slut. She hadn't told him about the time she and her sisters had discovered what the insides of their vaginas looked like, and, eager to share, had given demonstrations to most of the other kids in the neighborhood, lying on their backs in the prickly grass, pulling down their underpants, spreading their legs, and then separating the walls of their vaginas by pulling on their pre-pubescent labia. She hadn't told him that, when she was in high school, she used to think about becoming a stripper, if for no other reason than to give her mother a heart attack (only it had been her father, whom she actually loved, who'd had the heart attack, leaving her with a permanent sense that her teenage fantasy had somehow leaked over onto him, making her, in some vague way, responsible for his death.) She hasn't told him that once, when she was very drunk, she simulated oral sex on a banana on a dare from someone at an LSU frat party whose name she can no longer remember and whose face is a blur. She'd been a sophomore. Nor had she told him about her Jesus dreams. Because in her Jesus dreams Jesus isn't doing God-things like blessing her or enfolding her in His arms, but rather, doing guy things, like asking her to go down on him. Sometimes in the dreams she complies; other times she doesn't; but no matter what, she wakes up feeling like she's done something horribly, and shamefully, wrong.

Versus the kind of Jesus dreams that everyone at Hope House seems to have just about every other minute—dreams, visitations, visions, you name it, someone at Hope House has had it. Even Mr. Leon, who more or less looks like he's been run over by a truck and spends most of his days dozing, likes to talk about the time that Jesus appeared to him, one day way back in the long-ago olden days of his youth, and led him out of danger. Only that's not how he tells the story. He says: "Jesus dun come and took me by the hand, took me so's I know it was Jesus and not the Devil, and he take one look at me and say, 'Leon, we gawn get you outs of here.' And that's jes what he dun do. He takes me right on out of there, and if He hadn't, I wouldn't be here today to tell it, because where I was, down in the lower ninth ward, well that ole house, I was there doin' what I shouldn't a been doin, undustan? That ole house, jes one hour after I lef it? It go right on up in flames." If Annie or Dianne or any other of the care-givers happens to be around to hear Mr. Leon when he tells his Jesus story, they always supply the requisite solemn "amen," but to Suzette, the message is pretty straight-forward: back in the day, Mr. Leon did a lot of drugs.

But she reads to him anyhow—mainly from the Psalms, which bores her to tears. Sometimes she reads magazine articles aloud to him, too. Once she read a Flannery O'Connor short story, the one about the Bible salesman who steals a crippled girl's wooden leg, leaving her flailing around in a barn somewhere, with straw in her hair. Usually, no matter what she reads, he falls asleep.

But reading to Mr. Leon was still better than hanging out with, for example, Donny, who looks at her with the malevolent expression of someone who was planning on raping her and then chopping up her body parts and strewing them off the Mississippi River Bridge. Or the dreadful whining Yolanda, who loathes her, and made her feel, with every move, that she's doing something wrong. And that's another thing: she's never been either particularly vain or particularly self-conscious, but at Hope House she can't get it right: no matter how she dresses, her boobs and rear end seem to blossom into mammoth monstrosities, her skin turns a bright pale white, and her eyes, which are actually quite pretty, gray with a green tint, narrow to slits. Her father, the surgeon, had been a handsome man, and she looks like him, with thick dark brown hair cut short at her neck, a wide-open, contemplative face, and delicate ears like commas.

Actually, Donny wasn't any more troubling to her than anyone, or anything else connected to her work at Hope House. The truth was, the whole damn thing was trouble, though not in the kind of direct, indecent, lurid ways that her mother envisioned, involving Suzette's being infected by a black man with a big penis who, despite being on his last legs, overcomes her while she's driving him in her mini-van to the Dollar Store so he can buy himself a new deodorant and a pack of socks. She should never have told her mother Thing One about her work at Hope House to begin with, let alone admit that most of its residents were black. But—and this was the kicker—exposing her mother's hypocrisy and snobbery, her vanity and pornographic imagination, gives Suzette no end of sickening, petty pleasure. In another life, she thinks—in the life her mother would have had had her mother not escaped East Butt Fuck, Mississippi, and landed Suzette's father—it would have been her mother, and not Suzette, who would have thought about become a stripper, or, depending on how ambitious she was, an out-and-out porn-star.

Her mother, true to the cliche that she'd devoted her life to embodying, insists that Suzette would be happier and more fulfilled working for the Junior League. Not that there was anything wrong with the Junior League other than that its ranks were composed of mindless twits. On the other hand, being surrounded by mindless twits couldn't be any more boring than hanging around with brain-dead ex-cons and various semi-literate and soul-deadened junkies. Now and then, usually when she's returning home after one of her endless Thursday mornings there, she tries to rank what it is she dislikes most about the place. Is it the endless Jesus-thumping? The pathetic, inexorable march to death? The utter lack of self-examination? The seeming inability, even among those who are nearing death, to so much as entertain the notion that they may have crossed a moral line during their days of whoring, stealing, shooting-up, pimping, rob-bing, and/or murdering? Their simplistic notion that just because, you know, I dun killed a man, he had it coming, and anyway, Jesus dun forgiven me? As if Jesus is nothing more than the big enabler in the sky: It's all right, sweetheart, I know you are a scum-sucking unemployed lying thieving drug-addicted pimp, but I still love you—and by the way, since you spent your kids' milk money on getting high, here's a hundred bucks to tide you over.

Which are exactly the kinds of stories she hears every time she takes one or another of the residents out on their endless, tedious errands: like the story that Louis had told her about how angry his girlfriend had been when she found out that, in addition to his wife, he had another girlfriend (but it was okay because he'd repented); or the one Lucy had told her about her life as a street-walker and drug-hustler before she'd found Jesus and been washed white as snow. And on and on they went, every last one of them, utterly without guilt, shame, remorse, or even the slightest inkling that maybe, had they made smarter choices, they wouldn't be limping around with AIDS, living off the charity of the Catholic Church, and counting down the minutes until a "Little House on the Prairie" rerun came on TV.

Sometimes she played a little game with herself called "Who would you least rather be stuck in an elevator with?" Would it be worse to be stuck with her mother or with George W. Bush? Her high-school American history teacher—a hag with a monotone—or her little sister Polly? That redneck asshole Donny who stares at her chest or the dull-as-death Father Ralph? She gets no end of pleasure from playing this game, including in it everyone she could think of—kids who'd tormented her in school, bad boyfriends, foreign dictators, and really loathsome historical figures like Nero, Hitler, and Pol Pot. The only person she'd never put in the stuck-elevator game was the asshole who'd given her her pornographic nickname, and the only reason, she thinks, that she never put him in the game is because if she did, she'd have to hunt him down and kill him.

Wanda or Lilly?

The only one she did like, positively and without reserve, the only one she was drawn to just because was Annie, which, given that Annie was the biggest Jesus-thumper of them all, was weird. After all, besides their shared female anatomy, it wasn't like the two of them had anything in common, or anything to talk about, or even a single shared point of reference. What would Annie think if she knew that Suzette repeatedly dreamed that she was giving Jesus a blow-job? Somehow Suzette doubts that Annie would think that that was funny.

Suzette is giving her husband a report of the day's events, starting with Mr. Leon, who had developed a wheeze and whose hands, since last week, had become covered with ooz-ing sores, and ending with Miss Beatrice, whose middle-aged daughter had died, of cancer, over the weekend. Because the thing of it was: Miss Beatrice didn't seem particularly sad. Which is what she's telling Adam, now, as the two of them clear up the dinner dishes. "She just keeps saying that her daughter's in a better place," she says. "And you know, this daughter who just died? That's the third of Miss Beatrice's children who have died. There were eight in all. Can you imagine? And three of them dead."

Adam doesn't say anything as he goes from table to counter-top and back again. His wide white forehead glints under the electric kitchen lights. He has a nose like a potato wedge. From upstairs, she can hear what sounds like the towel rack falling to the floor in the kids' bathroom.

"When I told her that I was sorry to hear her news, she told me there was nothing to be sorry about."

It was true, too. Miss Beatrice's oldest daughter had died over the weekend, of cancer. And Miss Beatrice had showed up at Hope House like always, shaking her head and talking about how Jesus doesn't give you anything you can't handle, no indeed child, and though her heart hurt something bad, her daughter was in glory, and just as soon as Jesus called her up, too, she'd be seeing her. You just got to give your pain to Jesus, let Him handle it, praise the Lord.

"I just don't get it," she says.

"I think it's great, what you're doing," Adam says. "But I think you'd be happier if you went back to work. Not to mention that we could use the extra income."

Which is what Adam always says when she tells him about the day's events at Hope House.

"It's simply astonishing to me," Suzette says, "how Miss

Beatrice just keeps going like that, always cheerful, never complaining."

"You're not a social worker," Adam says.

Though she'd discussed it with her therapist, Suzette honestly didn't know why her mother, who at one point, probably for the first few years after Suzette's birth, had merely been shallow and vain, became, with the successive births of each of Suzette's sisters, dangerous and malevolent. As if "Suzette the Majorette" wasn't bad enough, she'd repeatedly called Polly "Roly-poly," and, when Polly was eight, had put her on a diet. She'd named the youngest of the three Gardenia, which in itself was a sin. As soon as she reached eighteen, Gardenia had changed her name, and now went by Francesca. It made no difference, however, as Gardenia-Francesca had still managed to have three children by three different men, and now lives on welfare in a trailer somewhere in Oklahoma. Polly on the other hand had married a real-estate developer, and has a ten-bedroom house in Houston, where she presides over big parties, and refuses to speak to either her mother or her sisters.

Shortly after her father, the surgeon, had died, Suzette had taken it into her head that, no matter how humble, she wanted to know what her "roots" were. Her mother had liked to talk about how, on her side of the family, they'd all been landed planters who had fallen on hard times. She threw around names, too: "You've got the blood of the Shelbys flowing in your veins." "Mamma's family were all Pierces, of the North Carolina Pierces, you know." Where her mother had picked up these names was something that

Suzette couldn't know, but she guessed that she'd simply made them up out of thin air. God knows that she didn't lift them from books, whose function, as far as her mother was concerned, was strictly confined to home décor. (What a priceless piece of luck it had been when Suzette's mother had bought the entire set of leather-clad "Classics of World Literature," arranging their gold-embossed spines just-so on the built-in bookshelves in the den.)   Suzette's mother's maiden name, which she'd only discovered after Suzette had badgered her father's lawyer's secretary to let her have a copy of his will, was Kott.

So she'd gone in search of the Kott family, finding, at the end of her journey, that just about all of them had died of the kinds of things that butt-ignorant poor people died of: lung cancer, heart disease, diabetes, and, in the case of one of her mother's brothers, a fatal car wreck. She met two cousins, pleasant-enough, overweight sisters dressed in nearly identical pantsuits. They told her that their grandparents had married young and had six kids, but that one of them had died when it was only a baby, they didn't know what from, adding that Suzette sure did have a cute figure, and wasn't it a shame how most women, themselves included, just blew up like blowfish once the children came along?

"I just don't understand," her mother, on the phone, was saying, "why you keep goin' back to that awful place. And I know for a fact that Adam doesn't like it, either." Which was bullshit, because even if Adam didn't have much enthusiasm for Suzette's work at Hope House, he can barely tolerate his mother-in-law, whom he regards as an annoying crack-pot, and avoids speaking to except when strictly necessary. "Y'all could go work for the Junior League, or work at the church, or take classes up at LSU, or anything at all, and here you go working with those awful people, doing God-alone-knows what, and how do y'all know that one day one of them isn't going to infect you too? How do you know that? It happens all the time, people tryin' to help other, less fortunate people, and then one day, all of a sudden, they wake up, only to discover that they're just as sick as the people they're trying to help."

"You're dreaming, Mother."

"I am not. I read all about it, just last week, in *People*. And then I saw something about it on television."

Suzette didn't answer. She enjoyed cornering her mother and then watching her mother grasping around for new lies to bolster her original non-truth. She was standing in the kitchen, drinking the last of the morning coffee, and trying to decide whether to clean up the breakfast dishes now, before she goes to Hope House, or later, after she returns.

"I did too," her mother now said, answering the accusation that Suzette had not, in fact, voiced. "It was on one of those television news shows—not the regular news, you know, but one of those news magazines."

"Uh-huh," Suzette said. She was already late. Not that it mattered when, or even if, she showed up. Except that if she didn't it was sure to turn out that one of the residents had

had some emergency shopping-need—that someone had run out of underwear or shaving cream—or that someone else needed to go visit his sick old auntie up in the hood, or worst of all, that someone needed a ride to Earl K. for an appointment at the dental clinic to get a new set of dentures or to have his remaining rotting teeth pulled, which meant that Suzette would personally have to go out with whichever resident it was, half-pull and half-carry him across the parking lot, deal with the invariably rude, overworked receptionist, find a seat, and try as best she could to settle the resident in for the inevitable day-long wait, leaving the resident to his destiny while she drove off in her ancient minivan with its "War is Not Pro-Life" bumper sticker that she refuses to remove.

"When," her therapist had asked her not long ago, "are you going to be able to feel good enough about the work you do at Hope House to be able to accept atonement, as it were, for what you consider to be your sins?"

Her mother said: "And on the show, why Suzette, it was just awful. I'm telling you. On it they were interviewing a woman, a nice white woman, not that it matters that she's white, but this was just a regular nice woman, like yourself and like everyone we know, just a nice woman, married and with children of her own, and it looked like she had been visiting her maid's son, or something like that, because he had fallen on hard times, and she was trying to help him, you know? Only it turned out that he had AIDS, because he'd been abusing drugs, and well, here this nice woman, just as nice as can be, had been trying to help out her maid's poor unfortunate son, and the next thing she knows, she's got AIDS too."

"What kind of drugs are you taking?" Suzette said.

"I am not making this up, and I have to tell you that I am sick and tired of your implying that I am. Your father, if he were still alive, he'd tell you the exact same thing I'm telling you, and he ought to know, too, seeing as he was a doctor."

"A surgeon," Suzette added.

"That's right, he was a surgeon, and fine man, and a catch, and here you are, you've got a nice husband yourself, and well, maybe Adam isn't ever going to make as much money as your daddy did, but then again, Adam's a lawyer, and not a surgeon."

"Dear God."

There was a slight pause, as if maybe Suzette's mother hadn't heard her right, or perhaps *had* heard her right, but didn't know what to make of the information. In any event, she plunged on: "And the next person they had on the show? Well, he was a what-do-you-call-it? A home-care nurse. The kind that comes to your house. And not gay, either, because they interviewed his wife and children too. A nice black man, real soft-spoken, like maybe he was a doctor instead of just a nurse, but even so, you could tell right away that he was a nice man, and educated, too."

This was another of Suzette's mother's pretensions: that she wasn't personally prejudiced or racist in the least, but that, as everyone knows, there was a world of difference between the nice, educated black people, the kind who you might even have over for a dinner party, especially if they were doctors or lawyers or if their wives were in nice professions like teaching or speech therapy, and the rest of them—

which included everyone who'd ever set foot at Hope House, along with the entire black community of New Orleans, Jesse Jackson, Jessye Norman, and the former members of the Jackson Five.

"And Suzette, y'all would just be mortified by what happened."

"What happened, Mother?"

"Well, what happened is exactly what you'd expect to have happen. That nice man simply up and died. He caught AIDS from one of his patients and no sooner did he discover that he was infected than he got cancer and died."

It was pointless to point out that the story was ridiculous on its face, or that Suzette's mother had contradicted her own preposterous story-line by giving her made-up nurse cancer, but Suzette tried anyway.

"You're a crack-pot," she said. "Half-baked. Insane. Beyond redemption."

"My little Majorette," her mother said. "You have the blood of the Pierces' flowing in your veins, and all you want to do is lie down in the gutter."

It had been a mistake, coming back to Baton Rouge like she had after college, when the truth of the matter was she could have gone anywhere, and done anything she'd liked, and spoken to her mother on the phone once a year. She might have gone to Europe to live, learned how to speak French and Italian, and worn silk scarves and big unusual earrings. She might have stayed in Boston, lived in a loft, and studied dance, which she'd been surprisingly good at, despite her heft, at Wellesley. She could even have become a professional dancer, the kind that dances for a few years with a small troupe in a small city before becoming an administrator at a community arts program.

"I just don't understand y'all," her mother said, breathing heavily into the phone, as if she were working on giving herself an orgasm. "I do everything in my power to teach you how to enjoy your life, how to find yourself a catch, and enjoy being a woman, and what do y'all do? You go squander it on that lesbian college you went to, and then by insisting that you have to be the same as all the men. It was that lesbian college that I blame, though."

"Do you know how moronic you sound?"

"Yeah, well, do you know who went to that lesbian college you went to? I was reading about it just the other day. Hillary Rodham Clinton, that's who."

"I like Hillary Rodham Clinton."

"Yeah? But do you want to know what else? Y'all's going to die of AIDS, that's what. You're going to get all sick and die, and then your children won't have a mother, and Adam will have to go out and get married again."

And that was another thing: if, as it turns out, she had to go return to Baton Rouge and enroll in the law school at LSU and marry Adam between the fall and spring semesters of her last year there, wearing a long-sleeved pearly dress that made her feel vaguely bloated, as if perhaps, as she uttered her vows, she'd metamorphosed into a perfectly rounded boiled potato, why did she also have to go and invite her mother to the wedding, when she knew, with the clarity of a prophet, that the only way she could possibly get married and enjoy it would be to scurry on off with a bottle of Champagne and a couple of friends to the nearest Justice of the Peace? But no, because at the same time that she knew that her mother's presence at her wedding could only ruin what should have been her day, she'd also desired—yearned—for a big traditional wedding, featuring a radiant bride in radiant white, a happy young bridegroom looking handsome in a tux, lots of flowers, smiling friends, and a mother whose only job on earth was to love her with the searing and fantastic intensity of the brightest, biggest star.

When she gets to Hope House, she learns that Mr. Leon had died two days earlier, which Suzette finds shocking, though she knows she shouldn't. After all, just last week, he'd been even more out-of-it than usual, more listless, his watery eyes more watery, his eyeballs more yellow, and his hands, resting on top of the bed covers, bleeding yellow-white discharge, as if covered with pimples. Already his things are gone, and a new resident has moved in, a tidy-looking elderly man with thick glasses and short, silver hair.

"Mr. Leon, he gawn to a better place, is where he's gawn," Miss Beatrice says.

"It was a real peaceful passing," Annie says. "One minute he here, the next minute gone. Just like a baby, falling asleep."

"Yes Lawd, and he resting in the arms of Jesus now," Miss Beatrice says.

"Amen to that," Annie says.

"Amen and amen again," Miss Beatrice says. "Glory hallelujah."

"He resting with Jesus."

"Amen."

"'And the LORD said: In the beginning was the Word, and the Word was with God, and the Word was God.'"

"Go awn, chile."

"Didn't He take away the sin of the world? And didn't He baptize the sinners, making them as white as snow?"

"He did!"

"And didn't He send down his only begotten son, his beloved son, the only begotten Lamb of God, and change the water into wine?"

"Glory, glory, glory."

"And didn't these things come to pass at Cana?"

"Jesus, Jesus, Jesus!"

"And didn't He speak of the temple that was His body, saying unto his disciples, 'verily, you shall destroy the temple, and in three days I will raise it up'?"

It was such a mishmash that Suzette couldn't really get a handle on it—Bible had never been much of an interest, and though it was taught by a leading scholar in the field, she'd thoroughly avoided studying the subject in college—but by then it was hopeless, as most of the other women who either worked for or lived in Hope House were present, and each one of them was adding her own version of the Gospels to the cacophonous stew.

"Glory be to God!"

"Help me Jesus!"

"Good news!"

"All the days of our lives!"

But just as abruptly as the impromptu church service had started up, it died down again. "Baby baby baby," Miss Beatrice was saying, giving Suzette's shoulder a little tap. "All kinds of people be looking for you. You got your van today?"

Suzette told her that she did.

"That's good, because lots of 'em, you know, be needing things. You know, first of the month, they SSI checks come through."

Which meant the usual: half the residents piled into her mini-van, their pockets stuffed with five- and ten-dollar bills, their hearts set on buying all kinds of useless, ugly gee-gaws and other things that Suzette simply didn't see the utility of—cheap little china statues of garden gnomes or bunny rabbits, hair-straightening products, velvet curtains, wind-up Santa Clauses from last year's Christmas season. She had a strong Puritanical judgmental streak in her, no doubt brought on by watching her wasteful, foolish mother fill her closets with enough inappropriately sexy clothes to clothe every call-girl in New Orleans, and stuff their house in Bocage Estates with enough gilt-tasseled curtains, plump, tufted ottomans, perfumed cosmetics, and expensive imported porcelain figurines to open a department store.

"Mind if I come too?" Miss Beatrice says.

Loretta spends a half an hour in the Dollar Store on Government Street looking for a track suit in her size (size huge) and some razors for her brother, a cross-dressing heroin addict who also lives at Hope House, but is too sick to go out shopping for himself. Elizabeth wants hand-cream, only she doesn't like the hand-cream at the Dollar Store, it was too expensive, which means that after the Dollar Store, Suzette has to drive to the Bargain Barn out on Florida Boulevard. Then she has to take Gordon up to the Social Security office to get a new social security card to replace the one that he'd lost when he was, as he puts it, living the life. But at least the Social Security office is reasonably close to the Walmart, which is where Miss Beatrice wants to go, to buy a birthday present for her one remaining, non-dead daughter.

That's where she saw him. At first she didn't think any-thing of it, or rather, didn't think that it actually was him—the asshole, who, during her second semester at LSU, had landed her with at least one of her vile nicknames—because she'd imagined bumping into him for such a long time that she assumed that the man in front of her, gazing at a rack of brightly-colored men's pajamas packaged in clear plastic en-velopes, was merely a not-very-accurate look-alike. But it was him all right, the guy who'd dared her to give the pre-tend blow job to a banana—ha ha, a big, drunken joke—or had she given the blow job to him? Even now, she can't re-member. And that's the other thing she's never told her therapist about: about how she can't remember exactly what she did do that night, whether she did it or merely dreamed it, like she dreamed about Jesus.

Fuck it if it isn't him, though, looking more or less the same as he had twenty years ago, when he'd been an under-graduate, studying political science. How can she remember that? She just does, that's how. She also remembers, as if by virtue of a memory serum misted into her brain by the buzz of the overhead fluorescent lighting, that his name is Hal, and that he'd had a poster of Elvis Presley on the wall in his dorm room, which Suzette had puzzled over, not knowing whether or not it was meant as an ironic statement. Now his hair, which had once been thick and black, is receding slightly, and he sports a moustache. He's dressed almost exactly as Adam dresses when Adam's not at the office, in beige Dockers, a soft, button-down long-sleeved shirt, and white running shoes.

She stands there, wondering what or what not to do, when he turns around, notices her noticing him, cocks his head, and says, "Do I know you?"

"I don't know," Suzette says.

"You sure look familiar."

"Do I?"

"I swear to God I've met you somewhere. Do you play golf?"

"No."

"Well, I've seen you somewhere." He smiles, evidently not put off by the sad little contingent of scrawny, poorly-dressed black people surrounding her like girl scouts. "I never forget a face."

"Oh."

"I forget names all the time," he adds, tapping the side of his head. "But never faces." Which was something she actually liked about living in Baton Rouge, the way total strangers would talk to you in places like the Walmart, joking and chatting about this and that and nothing at all, and then forgetting you the instant the interaction was over. But it was friendly, harmless stuff, the stuff of her own sentimental fantasies, and usually she joined right in.

"Looks like you got yosef a new boyfren'," Miss Beatrice, elbowing Suzette gently in the ribs, says.

"I guess."

"Now what am I gon get for my daughter?" Miss Beatrice says. "I was thinking maybe some nice perfume, but I don't know, things sho nuff is expensive these days!"

"How about a scarf?" Loretta said. "Me, I seen some nice ones at the Penney's, I still remember 'em, how pretty they was."

"Or you might could get her a CD. They got good CDs here."

"Or some of them fancy pretty soaps that come all wrapped up in a basket."

"Know what? Maybe she be liking those soft fluffy towels, you know, the nice ones that come with designs of flowers and butterflies and things like that."

"I don't know," Miss Beatrice continues, darting her monkey eyes around in her monkey-face. "I reckon I'll have to go and see what-all they dun got."

"You do that, Miss Beatrice."

"We ain't in no hurry."

Miss Beatrice takes a step forward, and so Suzette, along with her little army of sick, suppurating, ignorant, unschooled, illiterate, unaware soldiers of God begin to move on, too, past Hal, who apparently has resumed his search for pajamas. But just as they are about to round the corner to the next aisle and disappear into Women's Plus Sizes, Hal looks up, grins, and calling in their direction, says, "Now I remember."

"Ooo child, he remember you now," Miss Beatrice whispers.

"Suzette. The Majorette. Am I right?"

"He do know you!"

"LSU. I can't believe it! You read, like, everything."

"He remembers you good, girl."

But Suzette isn't listening, not really. Because how could she listen to Miss Beatrice with all those voices shouting at her from inside her own cranium? Do it, chew it! The roar gets louder now. She's going to faint.

"Oh God," Suzette says, out loud. "I think I'm going to be sick."

"You eat something that don't agree with you?"

"I need some air."

Her hands are clammy and her heart is racing and the voices inside her head have turned into a roar and all she sees is Hal looking at her with complete and utter recognition. His light green eyes are flecked yellow with amusement. He stares right at her, nodding slowly. She bends double, then collapses onto her knees.

"What is it, baby?"

"It's, it's—" But she can't get it out. How could she, without melting out of her present form, out of her skin and through her Gap corduroy skirt and pink cotton sweater, and becoming no more than emptiness and void, primordial chaos, motion without form?

"It's what, baby? It's what?"

They are all crowded around her now. She can smell them: Gordon's smell of apricot-tinged aftershave; Miss Beatrice's cigarettes and orange juice; Loretta's chemically sweet perfume; Elizabeth's cocoa-butter. All those smells, mixed with the odors of ragged breath and rotting organs, regret, failure, old age, despair, death. What's she doing here, with them? And then she remembers: she is one of them, a walking corpse.

"It's what, baby? What you want us to know 'bout?"

And finally, in a great shuddering sob, she tells them. "It's me," she says.

She could feel them all around her then, this little band of dying black people who she talks about with her husband and her therapist: they are all around her, like a protective shield, or like a warm igloo, or like a mother's arms, rocking her baby asleep at night, promising her that she is loved and protected, and that no harm will ever come to her, no baby, no my precious one, nothing will ever harm you, not while I'm alive.

FATHER RALPH'S VIGIL

The only reason Father Ralph is here today is to see Lucy, because yesterday Lilly had called him on the phone—something she rarely does—and begged him to come, saying, "I don't know if you can get through to her, Father, but you know, she is Catholic." She'd gone on, describing how Lucy was sneaking drugs into Hope House, and paying for them, she thought, the old-fashioned way. He'd promised to come by, expecting to find the girl curled up in her room in an agony of despair. Either that, or strung-out and sleeping. Instead, when he lets himself into the common room, what he sees is that they're all dancing, the whole lot of them, residents and staff alike, with Lucy right in the middle, her scrawny rib cage and high breasts visible through her skimpy t-shirt, and her face, usually so pale, flushed pink. He can never get over it, what he sees in this place, this hellacious, hell-hole of unrepentant vice. Yup, it's all here, in every variation and in all shades of the spectrum: lust, pride, anger, falsehood, violence, gluttony. Not to mention the ignorance in which most of them dwell, a virtual cesspool of darkness, the sticky swamp in which they immerse themselves as if it were the purest of glacial streams. Is this why he was put on earth? Is this why he was called to the Church—to minister to those who refused to be ministered to, to the unredeemed, the scum of the earth? How can Lilly stand it?

"The whole concern of doctrine and its teaching must be directed to the love that never ends. Whether something is proposed for belief, for hope or for action, the love of our Lord must always be made accessible, so that anyone can see that all the works of perfect Christian virtue spring from love and have no other objective than to arrive at love," he intones silently. But it doesn't help. Inside his ribcage, his heart contracts into a tight balled fist.

They're standing in a circle, chairs pushed back, waving their hands in the air as if they were at a rock concert, the women shaking their breasts and gyrating their hips, the men tapping their feet and pulsing with the beat of the music as if in the act of love. From the coffee table, a CD player is blaring Marvin Gaye. Or at least Father Ralph thinks it's Marvin Gaye. It's "Let's Get It On." He listens a while longer. It is Marvin Gaye, the one whose father, a minister, shot him dead. Dear God. Loretta is licking her lips. Wanda is shifting her entire ribcage from left to right and then back again. Even Lilly—who happens to be the daughter of a Methodist clergyman, which he knows because Lilly herself had told him so—is dancing, albeit with more self-restraint, her delicate frame swaying side to side on her small, paw-like feet. It distresses him to see her like that, looking, to his eye, so small and so vulnerable, so easily devourable, like a baby fawn. He himself has never been able to dance, suffering agonies at school mixers and, later, at weddings, and not just when he was forced to dance with one homely, awkward girl or another (his natural partners, it seemed, in life) but afterwards too, at home, in bed, when he felt ashamed and clumsy and deeply, fundamentally not right, playing and then replaying the tape of whatever had just transpired, the evening designed as if for his public humiliation. At the Catholic boys' school that his parents had sent him to, you had to go to the dances. That was the rule. And then, eventually, and no matter how hard you tried to make yourself invisible near the water fountain, some plump nun or well-meaning but emotionally-stultified priest would drag you into the middle of the dance floor and make you dance with a girl named Martha or Margaret, Suzanne or Brigitte, a girl with braces and freckles, or skin covered over with acne, or sweaty palms. The strangest thing was that these men and women, the teachers and tormenters of his youth, weren't even the slightest bit sadistic, either, but rather, he's come to realize, merely the victims of some sort of group amnesia, wherein the mind completely blots out one's adolescence, consigning it to the deepest reaches of the unconscious, there to remain buried until the end of days. He fingers his collar now, as if to remind himself that he's safe, that he never has to dance again if he doesn't want to—and that, indeed, the worst of his nightmares (his own death by AIDS, falling down a tunnel, losing control of his sphincter muscles in public), are merely the fantastical wanderings of his slumbering brain.

Scanning the room anew, he takes in Gordon, who looks

so healthy, with muscular arms and an upright carriage, that Father Ralph doesn't know what he's still doing here, a new resident named LaShara or LaShonda—he never can keep those made-up African-American names straight—Gordon, Loretta, and even Loretta's desperately sick brother, Bunny, who's doing a little dance in the confines of his wheelchair, which someone had moved into the center of the circle. Bunny. LaShoya. Where do they get these names? Once he counseled a little girl, couldn't have been more than thirteen, named D'Precious. D'Precious was knocked up but good, seven months gone, no daddy in sight, and a mother who, as far as Father Ralph could tell, was all of twenty-two. Ah well: the Deep South was a mess. Isn't that why he was called to serve here, when—truth be told—he could have gone somewhere—anywhere—else? He'd been second in his class at the seminary, with a bright future ahead of him, his choice of churches in need of spiritual leadership, and the hearty support of his supervisor and teachers. But instead he ended up being sent first to New Orleans to work with the poor and set up housing, and then, more than thirty years ago, to Baton Rouge—and all the homilies that during his years in Seminary he'd been preparing in his head shriveled up and turned into nothing more substantial than desiccated winter leaves. His fate was neither to baptize babies nor prepare bride and groom for the sacrament of marriage, but rather, to dwell, forever, among the sick and the dying, people who, more often than not, didn't even want his services. He can't even remember the last time he administered last rites.

Well, it's good to dance, he supposes. Better than sitting

around all day, watching TV and smoking. But what are the chances that Lucy will sit and talk to him? And even if she does, how could he—fifty-three years old, balding, fat, and all but a virgin—get through to her?

Usually, he doesn't come to see any particular resident, or for any particular reason, other than that, some ten years ago, his bishop told him to, saying: "In order to combat your own inclination towards pride, you need to do the kind of good works that will bring you to humility and gratitude." Only he didn't say it in such a high-handed tone, because that wasn't Bishop Price's style. But whenever he remembers that conversation—that directive—Father Ralph hears it as if Bishop Price was one of the stock characters that typically haunt the imaginations of first-year seminarians. He'd already been doing work among the sick at Our Lady of the Lake, serving as chaplain every Tuesday and Thursday, and then returning to the Catholic Life Center on the remaining days to do administrative work and lead the occasional (very occasional) youth program. But apparently—at least according to Bishop Price—that wasn't enough.

"Give me humility in which alone is rest, and deliver me from pride which is the heaviest of burdens. And possess my whole heart and soul with the simplicity of love. Occupy my whole life with the one thought and the one desire of love, that I may love not for the sake of merit, not for the sake of perfection, not for the sake of virtue, not for the sake of sanctity, but for You alone," Bishop Price had recited, apparently by heart, although with Bishop Price, who was something of a trickster, you could never tell for sure.

Father Ralph wouldn't have put it past him if he'd had some kind of cheat-sheet tucked up his sleeve or peeking out from beneath a pile of papers on his massive wooden desk.

"Thomas Merton," he'd added, just in case (fat chance) Ralph hadn't gotten the message.

"Father Ralph!" It's Lilly, waving from the dance floor. He gives her a thumbs-up.

"Hey, Father! Why don't you come and join us?"

"Yeah, Father. Show us what-all you got!"

He feels his entire chest, neck, and face flush, the heat building up under his collar. He would do anything, practically anything, if only Lilly were to disengage herself from the group and lead him back to the quiet clutter of her office. But she makes no move that would indicate any immediate plans to rescue him, instead continuing to do her little hopping dance, while one and then another of her charges, her cohorts, grins and beckons him to join the circle. Is this what Bishop Price had intended for him, then, that on every occasion that he sets foot in this place he'd be faced with one sort of humiliation or another?

"I think I'll sit this one out," he says.

"Aw!"

"You gon break my heart!"

"Oh Gawd, Father. Gawd isn't going to git on you if you have a little fun."

"It's good exercise for us old folks!" Miss Lilly adds, but he can hear in the forced joviality of her voice that she's not serious, and that, in fact, she may even be trying to find a way out for him. But before he has a chance to wave her suggestion away—either that, or run and hide—that big, vulgar simpleton Loretta shimmies towards him, wearing a bright pink, too-small track-suit, her lips covered with some kind of orange-colored lipstick, her wide hips and ample backside swaying, and her arms outstretched.

"Come on, Father," she says. "Get yo' groove on."

He'd heard—and it flashes through his mind now—that a month or so before he'd died, a man named Louis, who had lived at Hope House for almost a year before his T-cells all but disappeared, had had a dalliance with her, that the two of them had been caught going at it in the bathroom. Sex between patients is strictly forbidden at Hope House, but it happens anyway, as does every other vice, including drinking and taking drugs. Even so, Ralph had liked Louis, and had been more than disappointed when Dianne had told him what had happened. In fact, he'd been disgusted, the very thought of the two of them going at it like that, in a frenzy of lust, their eyes rolling back in their heads, their pelvises rubbing together, filling him with a kind of queasy disquiet not unlike the first glimmerings of an anxiety attack. And it's not that he's particularly uneasy about the concept of sex, either. After all, he's a man, with all of the usual lusts and passions, which, thank God, now that he's older, don't torment him as they once had. But they all break the rules: even Alvin, who's barely alive, sneaks alcohol and cookies into his room, and probably has whole boxes of Oreos and Little Debbie snack-cakes stashed somewhere under his mattress now, as if sugar might revive him. Frankly, Father Ralph prefers not to know. Though cookies were hardly illegal contraband, the house had strict rules about where you could and could not eat, formulated to keep roaches and other such revolting pests at bay. Ralph grew up in Chicago, hardly the Garden of Eden, but even after almost thirty years in the Deep South, he is disturbed by the robustness of the insect population. Surely when humankind finally extinguishes itself (as will happen, Ralph thinks, within a few generations) the roaches will take over the world, feasting on what's left of the excesses of human habitation—the garbage heaps and mortuaries, the mounds of hamburger meat waiting to be deep-fried, the vats of lard, the mountains of paper wrappers—and thrive for millions upon millions of years, eventually growing to be the size of dinosaurs.

"You know what I'm talkin' about," Loretta croons along with the CD.

Standing there, his face red, palms damp, bald spot shining, and stomach protruding out over his belt buckle, as it has, he's sorry to say, for the past two or three decades, Father Ralph feels the beginnings of a real anxiety attack, the kind that plagued him for years, until finally his friend Father Joe insisted that he ask his doctor for anti-anxiety medication, which he now takes twice a day, morning and evening, and which seems to help. But no anti-anxiety medication, no matter in how strong a dose, was designed to counter the onslaught of panic brought on by having a large, fat, black, HIV-positive woman shimmying up to you, pelvis-first.

"I don't think so, Loretta," he says, and at last—with hoots and howls from the assembled crowd—she retreats.

✳ ✳ ✳

"Yeah, so what is it, Father? Why you want to talk to me?"

He's alone with Lucy, the two of them seated facing each other in the small book-lined room off the lobby that no one actually uses, except sometimes to make phone calls. He briefly scans the titles on the shelves, and sees that it's mostly junk: Stephen King, Judith Krantz, and other authors he'd never heard of who've penned books with titles like *Flesh Tones*, and *Beach Boy*. Junk and junk videos. No Chaucer, no Shakespeare, no Thomas Mann, no Tolstoy—and for that matter, no Bibles either, unless you counted the illustrated Southern Baptist version of the Gospels. But what could he expect? No one at Hope House ever read anything more challenging than the TV guide. Some of them are barely literate, and those who are literate have no taste for reading. What they like to do is sit in front of the TV, eating potato chips.

Other than in the seminary, where he'd been a star student, and a favorite among his teachers, he finds it painfully hard to engage in any kind of conversation at all. Not that he's inarticulate, or unable to find the proper words to express even the most complex thoughts—far from it! In seminary, he'd been able to discourse and dispute at length on topics ranging on whether Saint Gregory followed the Rule of St. Benedict, and whether, if he did, what the effects of such engagement were on monasticism in England, to St. Bernard's devotion to the Holy Name of Jesus, to whether anger should be included as a primary sin. (He'd argued,

111

quite eloquently, against it.) So too, in his papers and homilies, he'd written with passion and clarity on any number of difficult subjects, from the mystery of the incarnation to Jesus' relationship to the Hebrew scripture. The words had simply poured out of him, entire rivers of words cascading together to form a deep and beautiful ocean, and he knew, then, that he'd been right to chose the priesthood—or rather, that he'd been right to listen to his better self, the Christ-within that urged him to take up his vocation. But now, faced with Lucy, he is as awkward and as tongue-tied as the most miserable adolescent.

"You okay Father?"

"I'm fine, Lucy, thank you," he at last manages to say, before lapsing back into silence. For God's sake, Ralph, he thinks: get a grip! You're not propositioning the girl, or even asking for her phone number! You're here to help...and what was it that I was going to say? For indeed, on the drive over from his room in the Catholic Life Center, Father Ralph had prepared his opening remarks, as it were. But all his carefully-considered sentences vanish from his brain. "Miss Lilly called me."

"Uh huh."

"She's worried about you."

"Well yeah," Lucy says. "I have AIDS. I guess that's something to worry about. And anyway, Miss Lilly ought to be worrying about her own self."

"What do you mean?" He shouldn't have said that. But if Lilly is in some sort of difficulty herself, shouldn't he know about it? Now, however, is hardly the time to ask. Lucy rolls her eyes. He tries again.

"Are you and Gordon, still—you know—still close?"

"You mean are we doin' things we shouldn't be doin'?"

Actually, that's not what Father Ralph meant at all. What he'd meant to ask is whether Lucy and Gordon were still such loving friends, as everyone in the house had come to realize months earlier, when the two of them started spending all their time together, either playing dominoes in his room (with the door open, too, so you knew they weren't up to anything) or sitting out back, just talking. Everyone had remarked on how beautiful it was to watch how, under Gordon's influence, Lucy had started putting on weight and joining in with the rest of them, like an abused child taken in by a loving foster family. But now any fool can see that she's getting skinny again and, worse, that her eyes constantly dart around the room, like she has something to hide, which, of course, she does. Yet she also radiates a so-what, in-your-face, don't-give-a-damn attitude that more-or-less has already annihilated him. Cold waves of what feels like electrified ice shards tingle up his spine and along his collar bones.

Father Ralph tries again: "Did you enjoy the dancing?"

"Sure." She gazes at a point in the corner.

"Is there anything you want to talk to me about?"

He waits to see if this last gambit, desperate as it is, will pay off, and sees that—duh—it doesn't. Lucy sits staring at a point in space near the corner, giving nothing away. Well, then. He'll just have to take the bull by the horns. God in Heaven help me get through to this child of Yours.

"Lilly—Miss Lilly—tells me that you're doing drugs again."

Lucy's small pink mouth opens into a small pink "o."

"And not only that,"—and this is so painful that he actually feels in danger of choking on his words—"but also, she suspects, she's not sure about any of this, you know, but she suspects, and she worries about, the possibility that you're getting money for the drugs in very unhealthy ways, and Lucy, you must know, if you're engaging in either of those behaviors—either the drugs or the other thing—not only will you lose your home here, at Hope House, but also, you are in the gravest mortal danger, the danger not just to your life, but to your future eternal life..." and here he runs out of steam, and sits, slumped over and covered with sweat, every cell in his body screaming to be released from this chair, this room, this place.

"Oh," Lucy says.

"My child," Father Ralph at last says, trying just one more time, this one last time before, he's sure, she'll either clam up entirely, rolling herself into a little ball of rage and hate, or start screaming, throwing a tantrum like an enraged two-year-old. "Surely you know that while your body was given to you merely as the outer garment of your soul, it was also given to you as a great gift—a gift intertwined with the gift of life itself—and that by taking any form of illegal drug, anything that can harm you, you are mocking that gift, throwing it back in the face of the Father." He breathes, heavily, waiting for her to start in on whatever ugliness, whatever verbal violence, is boiling within her. "And that furthermore," he says, wincing against the sound of his own ponderousness, his heavy, pretentious, long-winded, self-righteous phrases—worse than any nineteen-fifties headmaster or dry-as-dust, half-dead emeritus—"God is calling to you always. He is waiting for you, yearning, like a lover."

"Like a lover, huh?"

Blushing from the base of his spine, he continues nonetheless: "—Like a lover, indeed, waiting for your hand. Every time you do damage to yourself, He weeps."

"Jesus loves me, this I know, 'cause the Bible tells me so?" she finally says.

"Not exactly, but yes, he does. Love you, that is."

"Yeah, I've heard that before."

They sit together for a moment then, and now that his speech is behind him—now that he's actually managed to put some words into the space between them—he feels both more relaxed and more anxious, as if, at any second, some terrible scene is going to occur that he'll have no choice but to play out. (Where's Lilly anyhow? Isn't it time that she popped her head in to see how things were going?)

And now he goes out on a limb, his heart beating, his face flushed, his hands sprouting sweat, two little lakes forming in his palms. "My child," he says. "Have you taken your pain to Him? Have you asked Him to forgive you for your sins?"

Lucy shakes her head, no.

"Then you must do so," he says.

They sit in silence for a few moments more, before Lucy says, "I appreciate it, Father," and gets up, smoothing her miniskirt down over her small backside as she leaves the room.

✳ ✳ ✳

"I don't know, Father," Lilly is saying, wringing her hands in the nervous way she has whenever she's called upon to do something she doesn't want to do. Along with Dianne and Annie, they sit in Lilly's cluttered office, talking things over. Lilly, he thinks, is exactly the wife, or kind of wife, he would have chosen had he chosen a more conventional career: small, somewhat delicate, with the kind of extremely white skin that looks like it tears easily, and a small, pointed face that few men would see beauty in but which he finds stirring. True, she's not Catholic, but as the daughter of a clergyman she's sensitive to spiritual issues, and schooled in the Love of Christ, and surely, had she become his wife, and he'd asked her to, she would have become a Catholic. (Though at what cost, with a Methodist clergyman for a father?) Moreover, in Lilly he's come to recognize a strength and courage, a forthrightness in the world, that he admires beyond anything he can possibly admire in himself. How at home she is here, how comfortable with her staff, how at ease in this house of horrors! Truly, she is a valiant woman. An *eshet hayal,* as the Jews say in their ancient liturgy. And pretty in her own way, too, with those bright blue, merry eyes, her fading blonde hair pulled back, like a girl's, in a pony tail, and her delicate mouth. What must she have looked like as a younger woman? But what is he thinking? He's a priest; she's a married woman. Furthermore, a woman's life—her earthly life as well as her life eternal—is at stake. And what if the others were to notice the way he looks at her, staring while pretending to look elsewhere? "I've talked to Lucy until I'm blue in the face," Lilly continues. "We all have."

"That's right, Father," Annie says, adding, "Ain't that right?"

"Right as rain, but you know, it the old story. Some peoples they just don't want to take care of theyselves. It make you downright sick, what some of these peoples be doing to theyselves."

He likes the staff people at Hope House, and respects them for their fortitude and loyalty, their earnest human goodness, and their humble expectations (would that he himself were half so humble) but more often than not he's unable to fully take in what they're saying, not because he doesn't understand the lingo, the basic vocabulary of care and sickness, tenderness and compassion, but simply because they talk so fast, and with such thick black Southern accents, that he literally doesn't catch what they're saying.

"Holy Jesus in heaven, if someone don't stop that girl she gon stop hersef, and soon."

"It make you sick jes to think about it. And you knows, Father, and I hate to even say it out loud, especially to a man of God such as yosef, but you know, when she was on the street, before, she did them oral. The mens, that is. Right out there on Airline Highway. Hate to think that she doin' that again, jes when she finally begin to get well again. Jes when she doin' so good! That girl don have no love for hersef, not none. And poor Gordon, he aiming to marry that girl? I don't think so. All she'll do is bring him down, make him turn his back on Jesus all over agin. It jes break yo' heart is what it do."

All three women are looking at him now, waiting, he supposes, for him to either put a pretty pink ribbon on the entire (useless) proceedings, or suggest another way that one of them, somehow, might get to Lucy before Lilly has to put her out. But all he can come up with is: "God works in mysterious ways."

Unlike most of the men he'd gone through Seminary with, as well as the men and women of the cloth with whom he now works, Father Ralph has never had any one, particular crisis in faith, but rather, has had several minor-crises that feel more like a spillage from a cup of tea than like the entire cup being shattered. A drop here; a drop there—so many drops, so many spillages over the years that he's long since come to accept that his faith will continue to be challenged, regularly, if for no other reason than that like all mortal men, he is weak, prone to sins of heart, body and mind alike, and as needy, as desperate even, for God's grace and unbounded love as the most pathetic junkie, prostitute, rapist, or murderer. What plagues him more regularly, and with far greater pain, are doubts about his own vocation, which seems more and more ill-suited to him the longer he's at it, and which his regular visits to Hope House hardly assuage. It's not that he's opposed, at least not in principle, to serving there—and God help him if he isn't highly aware that the commentary running through his brain, that swirl of nit-picking voices and shrewish complaints, isn't the work of the Devil himself. He is, he knows, no better than the most miserable wretch wearing an adult-sized diaper and dying alone. Perhaps he's worse. Because unlike those who have embarked on their last stage in this life, he has never been shoved up against his own choices, his own free will, and his own end. Furthermore, he hasn't suffered sufficiently, at least not in the flesh: true, he has had his fair share of flu and colds, hacking coughs, and sprained ankles (he'd run cross-country in high school), but that's hardly the stuff that burns right through all your defenses, all the lies you tell to yourself, all the constructs of personality and ego you hold onto, and all your miserable sins, to get right to the core, the essence of the self, which is none other than Christ Himself: Christ in all His glory, beckoning us to serve Him. The heart of the mystery that is God. Nor is he better than the women who work there—not just the caregivers, but the woman who cleans, too, and that skinny dingbat of an old woman who comes from Volunteer Seniors, but doesn't do anything, or at least not that he can see, other than sit around and gossip—because unlike him, they truly serve in humility and awe, whereas he is always puffing himself up as some kind of superior creature, which—despite his education, his book-reading, his contemplation and meditations—he knows he's not. Not in God's eyes, anyway, which is where it counts. And as for Lilly...his Lilly—

He doesn't really love Lilly, of course; nor does he indulge in prurient fantasies, or even explicitly romantic fantasies, the kind that, were he to indulge in them, would put the two of them on a picnic-blanket under a tree, eating sandwiches, drinking Diet Coke, and talking about…perhaps about their childhoods, hers as the only daughter of a liberal Methodist minister in Ohio, and his as the only son of a devoutly Catholic and solidly prosperous family (his father, may he rest in peace, had owned a chain of shoe stores) on Chicago's North Shore. He can see them even now, Lilly's face dappled in the shade, his own collar loosened, as they swap stories, laughing. How in tune they are with each other! And how intuitively aligned! And what of Lilly's husband, anyhow? He'd only met him once, and that had been several years ago, at a World AIDS Day service, and hadn't been overly impressed. If memory serves him, Lilly's husband was a good-looking man, but overly-stern, and uncomfortable in his own skin. He'd talked too loudly and interrupted his wife several times, making the back of Father Ralph's neck itch. The two of them—Lilly and her handsome husband—have three or four grown children and a grandchild or two on the way, but more than that, he doesn't know, because even though he's been coming to Hope House for years, he's rarely spoken to Lilly about anything other than the tribulations suffered by the poor souls who live there. Only by asking her about the photographs that she keeps on her desk has he been able to garner what little knowledge of her home life he does have. Beyond those crumbs, he has nothing.

Nor should he, he tells himself as he maneuvers his car out towards the hospital, where his next appointments await. You have no business whatsoever so much as thinking about her, let alone indulging in these ridiculous, adolescent fantasies! Yet he senses something in her that calls out to him, calling out to him as if their souls were meant to be in some sort of communion...You're doing it again! Idiot! Fool! And where will all this indulgence in the realm of fantasy lead you? Exactly nowhere, that's where! Exactly onto the edge of despair.

As a young man, just starting his vocation, what had been hardest had not been celibacy (though God knows keeping himself pure had at one time been a daily—almost an hourly—challenge) but rather, the knowledge that his life would be, largely, solitary. Not that he had any illusions about the joys of marriage and family life, either. His own parents had been poorly matched, at best, and only by making the best of it, by throwing their shoulders back and fearing what might happen were they to do any less, had they made a go of it, raising himself and his three older sisters in comfort, but without any real warmth. It wasn't their fault either, the way each of them drained the warmth, the joy and spontaneity out of what he imagined must have once been a loving union. For had it not been loving, then why embark on it? Neither of his parents was particularly handsome, but they weren't unattractive, either. Rather, like most of the parents of most of the boys he knew, they were solidly-built, slightly doughy, trustworthy, and pale. Neither one of them would have been plain enough to worry about their marriage prospects, and in fact, as students, both of them had enjoyed a fairly lively social life, though it was hard for Father Ralph, even now, to imagine his mother dancing, or his father drinking beer with his buddies, two activities that both his parents assured him they'd indulged in regularly before they'd met and married. His mother had attended junior college only, learning stenographic skills, which she intended to use as a spring-board to youthful exuberance, envisioning a big-city life for herself, in an office, surrounded by other lively middle-class girls, the children and grandchildren of immigrants from all over Europe, and not just the Catholic countries, where her own ancestors had come from. (His maternal grandfather had told him stories about coming to America on steerage from Glasgow, Scotland when he was but a wee lad of fifteen.) Instead, just one month after she'd started working for an insurance company located, as she always put it, in the "heart of the heart of the loop," she'd met Father Ralph's father. The two of them had wed and immediately started bringing children into the world. By the time Father Ralph had arrived, in 1953, the White Socks hadn't had won a World Series in more than forty years, his father's business was booming, allowing the family to move to a center-hall brick Colonial in Winnetka that his mother decorated with dark wooden furniture and heavily brocaded upholstered pieces, his sisters were boy-crazy, his mother was fat, and his father was bald. To some extent, he was the child of their old age (forty and thirty-six being considered old at that time): his three sisters were already nearly women. He used to lie in bed at night and wonder how it was that his mother, who clearly had no great affection for her husband, was able to do what she had to do to produce him. His sisters, maybe—he could almost understand how they had been brought into the world.

(Back then, at a time when his parents had been more like the perfect lovers his mother was always reading about in the novels she checked out by the bushel-full at the Winnetka library and telling him about, all things, even love, were possible.) But now? Here in this house? Impossible.

She was an old woman now, with little memory of anything that had happened after the Second World War, living in a single room in a "special needs" home that the eldest of his sisters had found for her, where, apparently, she charmed the staff with stories of the snooty Northwestern undergraduates she'd once dated. When Ralph came to visit her, she'd look at him vacantly, and then say that she hadn't sent for a priest.

Ralph, however, had always wanted a family, and despite the torturous experiences with co-ed mingling that his teachers forced upon him at school, was fond of girls. His parents expected him to marry and father children, too—as they expected his sisters to marry and become mothers. All three sisters had, in fact, married and had families of their own, and now two of his sisters are grandmothers, with stories of all the cute things that their grandchildren are up to, and refrigerator doors covered with photographs of toddlers. It was just what you did, because even if the Mystery of the Incarnation was heady and alluring, and becoming an Altar Boy an honor and a mark of prestige, when you grew up you'd meet a girl, get married, have a family, and, along the way, help your old man out with the business, you're going to be running it by yourself before you know it, and frankly, that's how it ought to be, keep the family business in the family, that's what makes America strong. He can hear his father's voice in his head even now as he fiddles with the radio dial, trying to find the NPR station. It had surprised even him when he'd been called to serve.

It's a phone call for him, and coming in the middle of the night, he moves quickly. An emergency of some sort. Perhaps his elderly mother? One of his sisters? Hail Mary full of Grace. He hurries into his robe, shoving bedroom slippers onto his feet, because even in the worst heat of summer, the apartments where he and a few elderly monks live are cold. Though, these days, everyone has cell phones, there is only one phone in the building where he lives, in the communal kitchen. Telling himself not to panic—only when was the last time you spoke to Mother? Last week? And didn't you promise her that you'd try to get up to Chicago to see her? So what if she didn't understand a word you said? She's your mother, isn't she? —he reaches for the phone.

"Yes?"

"I am so sorry to be calling you like this, in the middle of the night." It sounds like Lilly's voice on the other end of the line, but just to make sure—just to check to see whether or not he's sleep-walking, and still unconscious—he says: "Who is this?"

"I'm so sorry Father. It's Lilly. Lilly from Hope House."

"Yes, yes, of course. What is it, Lilly?"

"It's Alvin. One of the night caregivers just called me—I don't know if you know Linda, she mainly works week-ends—but anyway, she said that Alvin doesn't have long at all."

"May Christ have compassion upon him."

"And anyway, well, and even I didn't know this, but apparently Alvin is Catholic, and he asked Linda if he could have last rites."

"Alvin is Catholic?"

"I swear to God, Father, I didn't know it myself. He always talked like he'd been raised, I don't know, Baptist or something like that, not that he was a churchgoer himself, even before he got so sick. The things you think you know about people and then learn you're wrong about! But anyway, and again, I hate to get to you like this in the middle of the night, but Alvin....do you think you might be able to get down there? I'm going myself—not that I can do anything for the poor fellow other than hold his hand. But you know what? Alvin and I arrived at Hope House the same week. First week of October 1995. It seems like a million years ago now, and I was so scared, coming into a place like that, not knowing if I'd be up to the challenges. And now I can't even remember all the men and women who've come to us. It's terrible, the way your mind blinks out on you. But anyway, about Alvin, well, I just didn't know who else to ask. It's okay of course if you say no. Alvin's not going to be alone. Dianne was with him all day, and Linda's with him now. He's spoken to his parents, too. He told them that he loved them. It was real sweet. Oh gosh! I just can't believe that Alvin's actually going to leave us."

"I see," he says.

"Some of them just get to you," Lilly continues, her voice breathy and warm on the phone. "But I'm talking too much, aren't I? I do that. But anyway, I just thought, I hope you don't mind, it's just—"

"It's fine," he says. "I'll be there as soon as I can. I just have to get dressed."

"You will?"

As if he could refuse. Had he not a sacred duty to perform the sacraments? Is that not why he had spent almost five years in seminary, studying, praying, meditating, and training himself to cleave not to his own needs and ego but to the Body and Blood of Christ Immortal? It's not about Lilly, he tells himself as he gets dressed and walks out into the night. It's not about being in the same room with Lilly. It's not about Lilly at all. A child of God is leaving this life. That's what it's about. Dressed, he swallows one of his anti-anxiety pills, figuring that five milligrams more of Buspar at two in the morning, or whatever hour it is, certainly can't hurt. Then he finds his New Testament, a bottle of Holy Water and a vial of oil, and heads out the door.

There's little traffic in the middle of the night, so he gets there quickly. In the parking lot, he notes that there are two other cars, which is good, because it means that Lilly has arrived before him. He wonders where she lives, and then wonders why he'd never wondered about that before. After all, it's hardly difficult to look someone's address up in the phone book. He might still do it. And then what? Would he drive by her house, hoping to catch a glimpse of her? And what if she saw him? But again, he is letting his imagination run away with him, when his sacred duty, the entire meaning and point of his life, was to be in the present, ready and able to carry out Christ's will in the world.

On the drive over, he'd searched his mind for an appropriate reading, but for the first two or three miles all he'd been able to come up with was: Jesus wept. *Jesus wept!* He was losing his mind. Five milligrams of Buspar? Please. Clearly it was time to go back to his doctor to ask about getting stronger medication. Finally, however, he'd hit on James, verse five: Are any among you sick? They should call for the elders of the church and have them pray over them, anointing them with oil in the name of the Lord. The prayer of faith will save the sick, and the Lord will raise them up; and anyone who has committed sins will be forgiven. Not that he intended to dwell on Alvin's manifold sins: God alone knows that Alvin had had time enough to make his peace. Alvin's not stupid, anyway. He knows what's happening to him.

When he rings the bell, Linda, the night caregiver, appears and together they walk down the short hall to Alvin's room. Inside, a single candle is burning—a nice touch, he thinks—and Alvin is propped up on pillows, breathing with great difficulty. His eyelids flicker open and then closed. On one side of him, Annie sits, holding his hand. Next to her is Lilly, sitting in a halo of light, her blonde hair glowing, as if electrified, and her pretty eyes cast downward towards Alvin's face. When she sees him in the doorway, she briefly glances up, and with the barest smile on her face, says, "Alvin? Alvin...it's Father Ralph. He's come to see you."

"Father Ralph?" the sick man whispers.

"I'm here," he says.

Alvin says something else, but his voice is so weak that

Father Ralph can't hear him. "He wants you to sit next to him," Lilly says. "He wants you close. You too, Linda."

Ralph approaches the bed, making the Sign of the Cross, and then moving immediately into Extreme Unction, starting with prayer, assuring Alvin that God hears all prayer, not only his but the prayers of all who love Alvin, and all in need, and even those who are in such need that they don't even know how to pray, or that such prayer is available to them. Then, reaching into his bag, he brings out the vial of oil, and blesses it anew. It's been at least a year since the last time he's done this, for an octogenarian spinster at Our Lady of the Lake, and now finds the ceremony to be extremely moving, so much so that he feels tears forming at the back of his eyes. Working the vial of oil open, he takes a moment to silently utter his thanks to God for allowing him to be here. But when he goes to anoint Alvin's hands and forehead, no oil comes out. Had it had dried up since the last time he had performed Extreme Unction? Father Ralph clears his throat and begins to explain what the problem is, but Linda is ahead of him. She gets up, pops into the bathroom, and returns with a jar of Vaseline.

"Here you go, Father," she says.

He takes it, and dabbing anew, says, "Let us join together in prayer," and as Lilly and Linda both bow their heads, every word that he had intended to recite—the beautiful words from the Gospel of James—fly out of his head, and all he can think of is Lilly sitting across from him, her hair down around her shoulders, her eyes closed as they would be in sleep.

"Father?" It's Alvin, whispering from his death bed.

"Yes, my child," he says, and tries again, "Let us pray." But again nothing comes out, and as the women sit with their heads bowed, and Alvin struggles to breathe, it finally comes to him, the exactly right, exactly most beautiful words ever written, or dreamed about. But before he has a chance to utter them, Yolanda appears in the doorway, as small as a child, with enormous runny eyes in her skeletal face.

"What's the priest man doing here?" she sobs.

"Go back to bed, honey."

"He ain't dying, is he?"

"Come on now, baby," Linda says, taking the girl by the hand to lead her back to her own room.

But Yolanda yanks her hand away, and with more strength than she can possibly possess, hurls herself on the bed next to Alvin.

"But I loves you!" she sobs into his ear. "Don't leave me! Don't leave me all alone!"

And in his great confusion, not knowing what to do or say, Father Ralph presses Lilly's hand into his own.

MR. WILBERT'S MISTAKE

First thing, he had to get his car back. His daughter had it now, but it was his, and he intended to get it back. He still had a little bit of money in the bank, unless his daughter had gotten her hands on it, which, knowing her, was a possibility. She'd been a cute little girl, but somehow she had grown up to be a mean and vindictive woman. Margaret. Kicked him clear out of the house, saying that she couldn't handle him anymore and all kinds of other things too, some of which weren't so innocuous, which is more or less how he'd ended up at Hope House, lying on the bed, because his legs were filled with fluid—his legs and belly both—and he didn't feel so good. Lying up there on top of the covers because once he'd made the bed he didn't like to get back in it, mess up the sheets. He'd always been like that: real neat. Even during his wild years, and he isn't proud of them, he'd been nearly fanatical about neatness. Couldn't much stand a messy house: no, there was no excuse for it. That was how he'd been raised. Which was another thing that had driven him crazy about living at his daughter's house: she was a bad housekeeper. Dirty dishes piled up in the kitchen; dirty laundry in piles on the floor; overflowing trashcans; a refrigerator crawling with mold; dirty toilets. Margaret's mother had not been a good wife, or even a particularly good mother, but she'd sure known how to keep house! Place was tidy as a pin, smelling of Lemon Pledge and cleaning fluids, all the pillows fluffed up so nice, it made him proud, having his friends over. But that had been way back, back in Washington, DC, where he was from, where he'd grown up and been educated, and where all his people were from, too. It was his home, and he planned to return to it. And just as soon as he could get his car back, get a little money together, he would. He wasn't going to drive the car though. He wasn't stupid. How could an old man like him, near-sighted and with swollen-up legs and a belly full of fluid, drive all the way from Baton Rouge, Louisiana, to Washington, DC? No, he was going to sell the car. He'd fly to Washington.

He's reasonably comfortable at Hope House, but it's only a way-station. He likes the way the women around the place fuss at him to eat enough, and to do his arm exercises, keep his strength up. Has his own phone; his own TV. But he doesn't much like talking on the phone, and as for TV, as far as he can tell, most everything that's on it is garbage. No: it wasn't like the old days, when people used to sit around and talk, when you knew your neighbors. Even in prison, people had sat around and talked. But he didn't like to talk about those years—he didn't even like to think about them.

TV and drugs is what had done it, made everything go from good to bad. That, and the way they kept pouring tax money into NASA, sending men into outer space instead of taking care of regular old Americans who needed help—the sick and the poor, people who couldn't get a job, or little kids. No, they just had to go spending your tax dollars on rockets that went into outer space, and then what? Nothing, that's what.

Which is exactly what he's trying to explain to Dianne, the nurse. Dianne is a large woman with a wide-open face, skin the color of copper, and a sing-song way of talking that reminds him of someone he used to know, though he hasn't been able to remember who. She stands in the doorway, leaning against the doorjamb, her arms folded over her massive, broad, comfortable chest. She is the kind of woman, he thinks, who in an earlier era would have been a wet-nurse, exactly the kind of old-fashioned Negro with whom the white folks would have felt comfortable, unthreatening, completely benign in her white nurse's shoes and her blue nurse's scrubs. Only of course she's not a real nurse at all. She's what they refer to as a "care-giver," which means that she has just enough education to keep track of medicine charts and dispense over-the-counter cough syrup.

"Ain't it the truth, though?" she says in her pleasant, Old South singsong. "Everything jes so wasteful now."

Not that she actually understands a word he's been saying, he thinks. So he tries again, this time with a mind to getting straight to the point. "You'd think that the government of the United States would have better things to spend their money on, that's all."

"That's true!"

"And our neighborhoods, that's another thing." He pauses, wondering, if for only a moment, what's going to be served today for lunch. Yesterday the choices were meat loaf and fried chicken, and he'd chosen the meat loaf, mainly because he thought it would be easier to chew. But the meat loaf had been a mistake, and no sooner had Wilbert finished his lunch than he found himself nearly bent-double with gas pains. "When I was coming up, we knew our neighbors. Fact is, we knew everyone in the neighborhood. People looked out for each other. Not anymore."

"Don't I knows it now."

"It isn't safe out there for anyone anymore. Not white folks or black folks neither, or young or old. Only where are the police? Where is the money to pay for the police? Where are our educators? Where are the parents? I'll tell you where: at home, huddled behind locked doors. And you want to know why?" He doesn't really expect Dianne to say anything, pausing, as he has, for rhetorical effect only, but she nods her head enthusiastically anyway, saying, "Indeed I do."

"It's because the politicians waste it!"

Just yesterday, in the paper, he'd read that NASA had sent some kind of newfangled space probe to explore Mars, or maybe it was Jupiter or Saturn, he couldn't remember. What he does remember was that the cost of the project was in the billions. Billions! Billions of dollars to send a computerized space explorer to the outer edges of deepest darkest nowhere, and for what? Because they didn't need to be spending that kind of money to find out what he, and everyone with even a shred of sense, could already tell them: that there wasn't jack shit out there, and there wouldn't be for zillions and zillions of miles—past the solar system and into distant galaxies and even then the chances were that you wouldn't find anything but swirling gas and dust particles and a void so deep and black as to freeze your blood and turn your bones to cement, and that no matter how many probes were sent to the great beyond, and no matter how much information it relayed back to earth, the great vast cosmos were as impenetrable to modern man as they had been to humankind's earliest forebears, walking on all fours on the broad green plains of sub-Sahara Africa.

"Isn't it something, though?" Dianne says. "And it make me so angry sometimes, too, especially when I see what them young people is doing to theyselves. Mercy, mercy, mercy." She shakes her head.

This was typical of the conversations he had at Hope House. He'd start explaining something that to his reckoning was as obvious as the existence of the floor beneath his feet, and whoever his interlocutor was would extract some minor point in the conversation and turn it into the main event. But that's how most of them were: good, but simple; kind, but uneducated. They got their information, such as it was, from TV, and only read the newspapers to see where the sales were. Even the social worker who was in charge, Miss Lilly, was like that. So were most of the visiting nurses. And those were the good ones, the ones who, before he'd taken sick, Wilbert would have considered, if not his equals in terms of understanding and attainment, then at least his equals in the eyes of God. Even Suzette, the white girl who came by once a week or so, and who obviously had some kind of education, didn't seem to be particularly bright, or even thoughtful, though at least she seemed capable of understanding subtlety. Then there were those (like the dreadful Loretta and the repulsive Donny) who were not, and never could be, his equals, no matter how you defined it. Father Ralph was in a category by himself. And finally there was Miss Beatrice. Miss Beatrice was a mystery, or to put it more accurately, his relationship to her was. Miss Beatrice herself was no mystery at all, but rather, as clear as water, as undisguised as rain. What wasn't so apparent was why he liked her so much, why, whenever she came by his room to sit with him, his spirits rose. Perhaps his liking of her had nothing to do with anything other than his age, and the way his mind sometimes played tricks on him, making him forget things he had said, or, conversely, making him think he had said something when he hadn't. Because it wasn't as if Miss Beatrice could even begin to keep up with him. She was, he thought, a woman of such limited imagination that she didn't even possess the ability to project herself into a larger narrative, or to conceive of herself as a singularity, a person with a path, a story, of her own. But that too was typical— since moving to Baton Rouge to live with his daughter, almost everyone he'd met, from both races, had possessed this vacant quality, this non-inwardness, this seeming disconnection with the world within. They were like children, or dogs, just going along, living in the here-and-now, cut off from both wonder and pain, past and future. As for Miss Beatrice, she reminded him, more than anything, of a squirrel busy gathering nuts. Everything about her was quick, from her quick little hands, to her quick little body, to the way her

sharp little eyes darted around the room. But she was also
utterly uneducated (she'd told him that she'd made it
through the tenth grade), and had worked most of her life as
a cook in a hotel, raising seven or eight children by two or
three husbands, and going to church. And that's what she
talked about, when she talked to him: her church, where she
used to be a member of the choir but wasn't anymore owing
to the fact that she'd been a smoker all her life, and Lord
have mercy if she didn't know she ought to quit, but she just
couldn't, and here she is, at her age—same age as Mr. Wilbert, and that was a fact—her singing voice ruined, and her
energy reserves diminished. Time was that she could climb
up and down all those stairs at the Hyatt Hotel, the old one
downtown near the river, and never once feel like she
needed to slow down and catch her breath, but those times
were gone and past, and now she needed to stop and rest
most all of the time, but praise Jesus she was still here when
so many others were gone, and as long as she was here, well
then, she was going to do her best to do God's work. Which
was why she came here, to Hope House, to begin with: to
do God's work. Mind you, she didn't have to do any kind of
work no more, not now that she was retired, and she has her
benefits, and the house was free and clear, and she had her
disability too, from what she got from when she was riding
with one of her daughters years ago, and was in a car accident, and had her hip smashed up pretty bad—Lord God it
was frightening, but I still here, and I still got breath in my
body, so as long as I still here I come to see y'all.

And on and on she went like that, every time she visited,

talking about her Bible study class, and her son who was laid out by diabetes and lived in a hospital bed set up in her front room, and her daughter who had died when she was only a baby, and her other daughter who had died soon thereafter, and the very last daughter who had died recently of cancer. She talked about her childhood as one of many offspring of a sharecropper and his seamstress wife somewhere up near Shreveport, and her first husband who was low-down, and her second husband who died of heart disease, and her third husband who she never actually married, who was the best of the lot until he started drinking, which was when she'd kicked him out, because by then she knew she didn't need a man in her life to carry on, not when she had Jesus. And anyway, she wasn't cut out to just sit around the house, watching TV and moping, because if God had put strength in her arms and her legs, and breath in her body, why, then, she was going to return the favor and work on Jesus' team. She wore a dark blue half-smock that came down to her waist with the words "Baton Rouge Senior Sunshine Team" stitched onto the top right hand corner, and a name tag bearing her own name. Her skin was the same color as his second wife's had been—a dark semi-sweet chocolate. He wondered if she was planning on coming in today. He wondered if the reason he was so fond of her was because she reminded him, however tenuously, of his mother.

His mother had been a maid. She worked every day for a white family in Cleveland Park on the other side of the city, a family called Lebowitz. They were Jewish, which apparently accounted for their having such a hilariously ridiculous name. Every day Wilbert's mother came home with stories about all the cute things that the little Lebowitz children did. There were four of them: three girls and a boy, all of whom were younger than Wilbert and his sisters. Now and then, she came home with things that Mrs. Lebowitz had given her: clothes that Mr. and Mrs. Lebowitz didn't wear any more, handbags, shoes, and sometimes even something really good like a piece of furniture or a china lamp. Once Mrs. Lebowitz offered Wilbert's mother an entire dining room set, a table and eight matching chairs, but it was too big for the small dining room on 17th Street, and she'd had to say no. And anyway, by then Wilbert's mother had saved up enough of her own money to replace the beat-up lino-leum table that had once been Wilbert's grandmother's, buy-ing a handsome round table of dark wood that gleamed like gold when the sun hit it, and never did have a speck of dust on it either, because that's what kind of housekeeper his mother had been. No doubt it was her example that at-tracted him to his first wife, Elizabeth, because Elizabeth had not only been a good housekeeper, like his mother, but she'd been an upright woman too, the kind of woman who still wore hats, and who didn't much approve of the way the younger people were going around marching and growing their hair into long wild frizz-balls. She'd been a cold-hearted woman, though, cold and mean when she didn't like what he was doing, cold to his needs, and downright nasty when she felt like it. She didn't much care for Jewish people, either, even though she'd met Mr. and Mrs. Lebowitz on more than one occasion, and of course knew that it was they—and not his hard-working, over-tired, old-fashioned parents—who'd paid for his education at Howard.

Mrs. Lebowitz was active in social causes. She spent a lot of time in Southeast DC, telling Negroes how to keep their daughters from getting pregnant. She also sat on boards. She was a dark-haired woman who'd talk to anyone and who, despite her wealth, drove around in an old Ford station-wagon that always smelled like dogs. She was overly-direct, the kind who'd go right up to you and say, "Are you doing well in school?"—as if it were any of her business. That, and she acted like she had a right to be loved by everyone, black or white, rich or poor. Wilbert's mother was devoted to her, and went around saying things like, "Mr. and Mrs. Lebowitz, they ain't like ordinary white folks, they different, they better. They don't look down on me, thinking that I'm not as good as they are. They kind. And the little ones, all them passel of little kids with their heads just full of curls? Just as sweet as pie." And she'd go on and on like that, telling them all how wonderful the Lebowitz family was, and how fortunate she was to have found such a good job. She liked Mr. Lebowitz too; he was an important lawyer. He knew Senators and Congressmen, and had even met the President. But it was Mrs. Lebowitz who she talked about all the time.

Wilbert's father worked as a janitor for the Department of Transportation. It was his job to keep the corridors clean. He wore a dark-green uniform and black work boots, and every now and again, he'd come home to say that someone important had passed him in the hall. Once, when Wilbert was already a grown man, married and out of the house, he said that he'd seen Jack Kennedy himself, but that was long before JFK had become President, or had even thought about running for President. He'd only recognized him because he'd seen his picture in *Life* magazine, along with all the pictures of all the other Senators and Congressmen who'd recently been elected and come down to Washington to run things. He came home every night with pain in his lower back.

It was Mrs. Lebowitz who told his mother that if young Wilbert could keep his grades up and get into Howard, why, then, she and Mr. Lebowitz would pay his tuition. Not his room and board (she said), or for his books or amusements (she added). A young man should have to struggle a little, she said—after all, even Mr. Lebowitz, who came from a wealthy family in New York, had had a paper-delivery route when he'd been an undergraduate at Johns Hopkins.

Only once had he actually seen the inside of the Lebowitz home, a big boxy place sided in stucco on a hill above Connecticut Avenue. He'd gone there with his mother one day when he was about fourteen or fifteen, to help Mr. Lebowitz out in the yard. Mr. Lebowitz liked doing his own yard work, and didn't want Wilbert, or anyone else, helping him with his flower beds, but he'd asked Wilbert if he wouldn't mind coming over to help him rake and prepare the place for winter. When Wilbert went inside to use the bathroom, he finally saw the domain that was his mother's world—the real world, or so it had struck him, the one where enchantment and delight, cleanliness and order, ruled, and not the dreary cramped over-heated world that the rest of them inhabited on 17th Street. Just for starters, the kitchen was nearly triple the size of his mother's kitchen at home, and flooded with light, the light just pouring in from large windows over the stove, which itself was a wonder, sleek and as big as an ice-box. Wilbert had never seen such a thing before. The rest of the house was like a fine hotel, with every sofa and chair plumped up and plush, covered with flowery fabrics in bright, cheerful, intensely vibrant colors: red and green, pink and blue. It was like walking into a flower garden. It smelled good, too. It smelled of air, and of light, and of something that he couldn't pin down that had to do with being white. The bathroom where he finally emptied his bladder was crouched under the stairs—he later learned that Mrs. Lebowitz referred to it as the "powder room"—but it too was enchanted, with striped wall-paper, and toilet paper that slid off a gold-colored holder like ribbon. He felt self-conscious emptying his bladder into that refined, white bowl, and when he was finished, he carefully inspected the rim to make sure that he hadn't inadvertently sprinkled so much as a drop of his urine onto the pure and perfect porcelain, dabbing at the tip of his penis with toilet paper to wipe off any remaining moisture just to be sure. But then he had an additional problem--what to do with the square of toilet paper? The only solution was to dispense of it in the toilet, and flush for a second time. But that would potentially mean calling attention to his bathroom habits, even raising suspicion. If he disposed of it in the trash can (another rare object, of black lacquer), someone—most likely his mother, but not necessarily—would see it there. He finally stuffed the soiled paper into his pocket. Later his mother told him that the powder room was for guests, and that she and others who worked in the house, including the driver who took Mr. Lebowitz to work, always used the bathroom that was off the basement playroom.

The miracle of it was that he'd gone on—without resentment, without rebellion, without bitterness or cynicism of any kind, doing exactly what his parents told him to do, and never giving either one of them any real trouble. College had been a gift so large that he could never repay it. He'd saved money by living at home, paying for his books with the money he made working in the summer. When he'd finally graduated (magna cum laude in English, with half a novel about the friendship between a black man and a white man in turn-of-the-century Virginia tucked away in a manila envelope), the entire Lebowitz family, including the four curly-headed Lebowitz children, had been in attendance.

"Now young man," Mrs. Lebowitz had said. "You are officially a member of the educated classes. What do you propose to do with yourself?"

"Tell them, Wilbert," his mother urged. "You have nothing to be ashamed about. Nothing at all."

"I hope to be a writer, ma'am."

Mrs. Lebowitz had given him one of her purposefully frank, unwavering looks, as if to declare that she knew her way around the world, and it was no use pulling the wool over her eyes, because even though she was rich and white, and getting older—even though her world was as removed from his as Turkey was from Tennessee—she could see straight into his soul.

"What kind of writing, Will? Journalism? Perhaps as a reporter for one of the Negro weeklies?"

His mother, wearing a new dark-red suit, stood by his side, gazing up at his face with the look of adoration that she usually reserved for the Lebowitz children. She looked like a giant overripe tomato with its woody stem still attached. Mrs. Lebowitz, on the other hand, was cool and elegant in dark gray, with a dark gray hat propped on her salt-and-pepper hair. Her husband, the lawyer, stood beside her, and their four children fanned out behind them, in varying postures of boredom.

"I aim to be a novelist, ma'am," he said, whereupon his mother, usually so reticent, popped in with, "And he's already written an entire book. Ain't that right, son? And he's shown it to his professor and all, a professor of—what did you say, Wilbert? Modern American literature, that's it, and his professor, he say—" But at this point Wilbert couldn't much bear it any longer, and clearing his throat, said, "Mamma!"

Mr. Lebowitz smiled. Wilbert's mother looked around, confused. But she soon rallied.

"You're right, son," she said, adding, for the benefit, he supposed, of the Lebowitz clan, "Wilbert has always been so modest!"

"I had a cousin who fancied herself a writer once," Mrs. Lebowitz said. "Cousin Jenny. From St. Louis. She wrote poetry."

"Yes ma'am."

"Do you write poetry, Will?"

"No ma'am."

She nodded, approvingly, but an unpleasant sensation opened up deep inside him, the first glimmerings of what would turn out to be a secondary, but virulently potent, truth. More than anything, he wished that he had never told his mother the first thing about what he was studying, and who he was reading, and what he was doing in college. It would have been better if he'd confined himself to merely telling her the basics—that he liked his studies, that he was working hard, that he was getting good grades—and left it at that. But he hadn't. Instead, just about every night after the dinner dishes were cleared up and before he went upstairs to study, he'd sit in his mother's kitchen, drinking her coffee, and telling her every little last detail of his dreams and ambitions. He'd even told her the name of his half-finished novel: *Mr. Lester's Hope.* And she'd gotten it wrong, anyhow. The manuscript was far from finished, one, and two, he never had gotten around to showing more than the first chapter to Dr. Templeton. At least he'd kept one thing to himself, which was no more or less than the discovery of who, and what, he really was, and the shiny, bright, magnificent and pleasant future that already was opening up before him.

Mrs. Lebowitz had made him feel like he was both invisible and transparent, like she could see right through him, right into the core of his being, where he stored his secrets, his pride, his ambition, and his shame. Perhaps it was because she was a Jew. But the opposite was true at Hope

House. Other than the fact that he was an older, educated man, no one knew the first thing about him. They knew nothing of his past other than what they might surmise by his condition. They looked up to him, too, as well they might, and even came to him, on occasion, for advice. Where to find a lawyer. (Legal Aid.) Whether it was worth voting for the President of the United States when everyone knew that no President would ever help out black people, especially poor black people down in the Deep South, and that was a fact. (Vote anyway, he said.) What kind of car to buy. And so on. What they didn't know, however, was pretty much everything about him, and from time to time he wondered what they'd think if they knew that he had sunk as low as any man here. Seventeen years at Greenville. But then he puts it out of his mind. He'd served his time.

His toes are beginning to tingle the way they do sometimes when his legs are going numb. That would be the fluid, again. The fluid that's all backed up in his body, giving his cheeks a roundness that they didn't formerly have, swelling up his belly like a pregnant woman's, and filling his legs like two bloated sausages. It's morning, the light blue sunshine pouring in through his window, the grass in the garden outside turning a dark spring green.

"What's for lunch today?" he asks Dianne, who still stands in the doorway, her legs spread solidly beneath her.

"I's gon have to check for you on that, but I'm thinking the choice is gon be red beans and rice or smothered chicken."

"Which do you recommend?"

"Me? I likes the red beans and rice," Dianne says. She

cocks her head in a gesture of harmless flirtation, like the flirtation that goes on between a mother and her little boy. "But sometimes it can be kine of hot. You likes Louisiana cooking, Mr. Wilbert?"

He pauses for a moment, thinking about his mistake of yesterday. You'd think that in a place where everyone was sick the culinary choices would be more suitable. "I'll have the chicken," he says.

The boredom, of course, was dreadful: listening to Wanda, the cleaning lady, mopping the floor; waiting for dinner, and then for breakfast again; hoping that his daughter, who had a hard heart, might come to visit him. But at least, unlike every other resident, he could read. Institutional living didn't bother him much, anyway, not after Greenville. He wondered when Miss Beatrice would come to see him today, and then wondered if he should make the effort to get up to see if she'd already arrived, and was perhaps sitting outside, on the smoking deck, talking.

Instead the person who knocks on his door, pokes her head in, and plops herself on the chair in the corner is the white girl, Suzette. The one who, every time she comes to visit, re-introduces herself, as if perhaps he couldn't remember from one moment to the next who or where he was, or that other people also existed. She has an eager expression on her face, as if she were expecting an important phone call.

"How you feeling today?" she asks. Something about her reminds him of Mrs. Lebowitz.

Mrs. Lebowitz had called his mother "Judy," his father "Henry," and himself "Will." They called her "Mrs. Lebowitz." Even on her deathbed, his mother had been unable to call Mrs. Lebowitz anything other than "Mrs. Lebowitz," which Wilbert knew for a fact, having been there. It had just been the two of them, actually—himself and Mrs. Lebowitz—along with his mother, who was lying in the same bed she'd slept in for as long as Wilbert could remember, barely conscious and breathing with difficulty. Mrs. Lebowitz looked poorly herself, age having overtaken her sharp, knowing features and turning her once-dark hair a thin, bright silver. There were age spots on her hands and neck, and where once she'd worn carefully-tailored skirts, now she wore the same kind of formless polyester slacks that he saw women wearing in the grocery store. Mr. Lebowitz had Alzheimer's, and the four adorable Lebowitz children had all grown up and had children of their own, some of whom had turned out just fine, but others of whom weren't fine at all, doing drugs and getting into all the same kinds of trouble that kids these days got into, and speaking of trouble, wasn't it a shame that Mr. and Mrs. Lebowitz's only son, Allen, had so many problems? The boy's on his third wife already and now it turns out that he's had a drinking problem practically from the beginning and not a one of his wives was a nice Jewish woman like his mother, and Mr. and Mrs. Lebowitz hadn't liked that at all, and poor Mrs. Lebowitz, never did nothing but good in all her life, and worried about Allen as if he were still a little boy, instead of a man well into his fifties.

Mrs. Lebowitz, holding his dying mother's hand, had looked warily over the bed covers at Wilbert, who sat opposite her, near the wall on the other side of the bed. Pursing her lips, she said, "I want you to know that Mr. Lebowitz and I were very sorry for your difficulty." She breathed audibly, her chest moving visibly under her shapeless, long-sleeved blouse. "And we wanted you to know that we've had our own difficulties." The son, he thought—the family screw-up, Allen. "Life is full of surprises."

Then, suddenly, from the bed, a slight shudder, and his mother was talking. "Is that you, Mrs. Lebowitz?"

"Hush now, Judy," Mrs. Lebowitz said. "Conserve your strength. I'm not going anywhere." Then, turning again to Wilbert, she said: "I've told your mother a thousand times to call me 'Jane,' but no, she just won't do it, stubborn as a mule, even now. Just look at her, the dear old thing."

And he did. Or rather, he continued doing what he had been doing, which was gazing at her from an enormous mental distance, as if she were a likeness of his mother, rather than his mother herself. From his side of the bed, he noticed that his mother's chest was rising and falling more and more slowly, and that, on her side of the bed, Mrs. Lebowitz sat on what had once been his mother's best chair. His sisters had come by earlier, and were planning on stopping by again on their way home from work, but for now it was just himself and Mrs. Lebowitz, sitting vigil. His father had died, of massive stroke, not long after Wilbert had begun his incarceration. Now his mother's face, which for most of his life had seemed to define everything that was both right and good on the one hand, and denied to him on the other, was as placid as a puddle. In great old age, the flesh that had given her face its perpetual expression of resigned affection had fallen away, revealing the sharp, regal bones beneath.

"Isn't she just beautiful?" Mrs. Lebowitz had said.

And that's when it dawned on him, as monstrous, as toxic, as anything that he himself had done, bigger even than his own mistake, and in some ways deadlier. Mrs. Lebowitz really did love his mother.

"Do you take *The New Yorker*?" Mrs. Lebowitz said.

"I'm afraid I don't."

"Well, of course it's gotten worse in recent years. I keep thinking that I'm going to drop my subscription, but then, every once in a while, they manage to publish something quite good."

He wondered when his sisters were going to show up. But it was only mid-afternoon—the sun still high in the sky, orange-gold light beaming into his mother's cramped, shabby bedroom.

"The reason I mention it," Mrs. Lebowitz continued, "is because there was recently a quite wonderful short story, kind of rough, but very moving, by the novelist Leon Forrest. A prison story. He wrote *Divine Days*. Do you know it?"

Wilbert inclined his head in a gesture that he hoped would convey the word "no," which suddenly seemed like too much to ask him to say aloud.

"Too bad," Mrs. Lebowitz said, her old, no-nonsense, in-your-face briskness flaring up. "A wonderful book. Long, but so rich. I highly recommend it. A black writer, you know, and just really really good."

"I'll look into it," he said.

A moment later, his mother began gasping for air, her breathing becoming ragged and painful. He took her other hand—the hand that Mrs. Lebowitz didn't have—and squeezed it. "Mother, mother," he said, while, on her side of the bed, Mrs. Lebowitz was saying, "That's it, darling, that's right, you're fine, sweetheart, you're going to Jesus, you're going to see your darling Henry, that's right, he's waiting for you, and you're going to see your mother and daddy, and Granny Stokes, and Grandpa Abraham, they're all waiting for you in heaven, that's it, that's my precious girl, Jesus is waiting for you sweetheart, there's nothing to be sad about." And on and on she went like that, in her cool, low-pitched, educated, upper class Jewish voice, naming the names of Wilbert's own ancestors, that group of gape-mouthed, oppressed, and dirt-poor Negro farm hands his mother told stories about, and talking about Jesus as if she gave a crap, until at last his mother took one last long raggedy breath, opened her eyes, and fell back on the pillow, dead.

"So what's going on with you today, Mr. Wilbert?" It's Suzette. For a second, he'd nearly forgotten about her, but here she is, still seated in the chair in the corner by his bed. She's wearing blue jeans and an over-sized, button-down shirt. "Anything I can do for you? Need me to buy you something or something like that? Or anything else? I'm probably going out later, with some of the guys, if you need something."

"Can't say I do, but thank you."

She puts one hand over the other in a gesture of supplication.

"Still trying to get yourself back to Washington?" she says.

"I aim to."

"Nice city," she says. "Washington."

"Yes, indeed."

"But I don't know." She leans the top half of her body into the back of the chair, pushing a lock of straight brown hair away from her eyes. Again he wonders what she's doing here.

"What don't you know?"

"I don't know about Washington," she says. "Not for you, personally. I mean, it's a nice city. Big and pretty. But what the hell kind of government have we sent there? Me? Personally? I'm sick to my stomach, just thinking about it."

It comes back to him now. Suzette is the one who likes to talk about politics, about things she's read in the newspaper. She's the one who, during the elections, had gone on and on about asserting your right to vote, nagging the residents who weren't registered to get registered, and driving people to the polls.

"It's the waste that gets to me," he says. "Like this space program of theirs, and here there are so many people in need. People dying in Iraq but things in America aren't so good either, and what are they doing with our tax money? Sending rockets to Mars."

"And you want to know something else? This gang they have now? I'm not saying that they're personally racist or anything like that. But you know they don't give a shit about poor people."

He'd never met a white liberal outside the Lebowitz family until he was out of prison, and back in Washington, this time working at a half-way house for other newly-released prisoners, where he taught basic job and literary skills, and tutored, on the side, in a high school. But at Hope House, all the white people, including the Catholic priest who stops by now and then, were liberal, something he finds slightly ludicrous, though he doesn't know why.

"I have to agree with you there," he says.

It's the end of the conversation. But Suzette just sits there, in the room's one chair, with that quizzical, determined expression on her face that reminds him of Mrs. Lebowitz. "Sure you don't want anything?"

"Nope."

"Mr. Wilbert," she finally says. "How on earth did you end up here?"

"That's a very long story."

"If you want to tell me, I'd be happy to hear it," she says. She probably would be, too, and for a moment he considers how gratifying it might be to unveil the story of his life, starting of course with his childhood in Washington, and moving on up through Howard, his early career, and the mistake that had landed him at Greenville. Indeed, it had the makings of an absolutely dandy story, and he himself had thought more than once that he ought to write it, if not in novel form, then as a memoir.

"I'd rather not."

"But I still don't understand. How'd you end up in prison?" she says.

"I beg your pardon?"

"Last week—" she begins to explain, but her explanation is unnecessary. "Remember what we talked about?"

"What do you mean?"

"You told me you'd done time."

"I did?" he says.

"You were telling me about your career. How it got interrupted when they set you up. I still can't believe that kind of injustice."

Now he remembers.

"Racism was all it was," he says. "The way it was then, if you were black and educated, they had it in for you."

"But what were you charged with?"

"I'd rather not talk about it," he says again.

Shrugging, she tells him that she understands.

Usually he joins the others for lunch in the common room—the "lobby" they sometimes call it—but today he just didn't feel like it, choosing instead to eat by himself in front of the midday news. The chicken is bland, and the accompanying carrots are over-boiled, but he isn't picky. In any event, he doubts that today's chicken would constitute a problem. Just before lunch Beatrice had popped her head in and said that she hadn't forgotten him, and that she'd be coming in to talk soon, but so far she hasn't. Over the sound of the news he can hear voices swelling and then falling from around the corner.

He wishes that there were someone from among the residents whom he might feel close to, but there isn't, and there's nothing he can do about it. Most of them had hardly so much as left the state of Louisiana, and some of them hadn't even been outside East Baton Rouge parish. Worse, those who had gotten themselves into trouble, or landed in jail—and that had to be fully half of them—still seemed to have no concept of what they'd done. Whereas he'd spent the past thirty-six years or so—ever since he was first incarcerated in the DC jail—thinking about his own mistake, and wondering what his life would have been had he not made it. In prison, he'd read everything he could get his hands on to try to make sense of it, reading and then re-reading Shakespeare—*Macbeth, Othello, Hamlet, Lear*—in search of some clue to his own sad life. He'd tackled Marcus Garvey, Charlotte Bronte, and Edgar Allan Poe. He'd even read the Bible.

"You wanting to be seeing me?"

At last, it was Miss Beatrice—Beatrice—dressed, as always, in slacks, sneakers, and the dark-blue "Baton Rouge Senior Sunshine Team" smock that made her look like an overage girl scout. Her curly hair frizzed around her head like black electricity.

"Where you been?"

"Oh now, you would ask me that, wouldn't you? As a matter of fact, I been out with my boyfriend."

"You strike me to the quick."

"And I aim to have myself a good old time, too!"

With that, she allows herself to be drawn into the room,

where she takes the same seat that Suzette had occupied earlier. All the bedrooms here are the same, furnished with a hospital bed, a standard-issue hospital-type easy chair, and a dresser, with a bulletin board on the wall, an open-style closet, and a single window covered with colorless blinds. Some of the residents have filled their rooms with all kinds of personal possessions—quilts and framed photographs and pillows and knick-knacks—and stuffed their closets with clothing and shoes. But Wilbert has always been a man of modest tastes and simple needs, and so the sparseness of his surroundings, if anything, gives him a sense of order. The one thing he does have is books, but even these he keeps neatly, in stacks along the wall.

"So what do you know good today, old man?"

"You tell me."

Squirrel-like, she props her tiny, bony body forward on the chair, and says, "Well, for one thing, a little bird told me something about you."

"And what little bird would that have been?" he says, thinking naturally of Dianne, and their conversation of this morning, or perhaps of his daughter, Margaret, who keeps saying that she is going to come to visit him, and then never does. It is entirely possible, however, that—in the way of the world—Miss Beatrice had met his daughter, and gotten to talking to her. Baton Rouge was a small town. Everyone knew everyone. "Was it, perhaps, a little bird who works here at Hope House?" he says.

"Now you know I ain't gon be telling you what little bird's been chirping in these old ears." With both hands, she points to her ears lobes, off of which small green globes hang like Christmas ornaments.

"Well then," he says. "I guess we'll have to change the subject. How is your son?"

But for once, she foregoes the subject of her son, plunging on, instead, in her own direction. "You ain't dun tol me that you served time in prison!" she says.

Looking at her sitting there, her mouth tight like a ball of string, he is hurdled back into an earlier time—the time, perhaps, that he was newly released from Greenville, and had to face his family again, or perhaps even earlier, when he was trying, and failing, to establish himself as a writer—and like then, shame floods him, starting at his bladder, and moving up into his throat and neck.

"But that ain't the point," she continues. "Because you and me are friends, right? So that's what I want to tell you. I want to tell you that no matter what you dun do, you okay with me. And what's more important, and you already knows this, you okay with Jesus. Not just okay. Jesus love you, baby. Not a bird fall out of the sky without Jesus be knowing about it. You know that, right?"

He's about to make some reply to this, something that will simply brush the subject away—and damn if he shouldn't have guarded his business, and why, of all people, had he mentioned his stay at Greenville to Suzette? But in fact he knows exactly why he'd told her: he'd told her because, in some bizarre way, he'd wanted to impress her. He'd wanted to impress her with his erudition on the one hand, and the mystery of his past on the other. He'd had some vague idea that the juxtaposition of the two, the way the two halves didn't add up, would jolt her into recognizing that he wasn't just any old black man, broke, sick, and stuck at Hope House.

Miss Beatrice, her eyes trained on him, is still waiting. "You have asked Jesus to forgive you, haven't you?"

He looks at his fingernails. Ask Jesus for forgiveness? Jesus should be asking him for forgiveness, and not the other way around. Because why else had Wilbert's life turned out the way it had, his beautiful, precious talent, all his blossoming potential, just withering away like that, withering away into nothing but wistfulness? Oh, his life hadn't been a total failure: even at his most miserable, even when he was newly arrived at Greenville and looking at twenty years, he'd enough sense of his inner self, his core being, and his intellect to keep himself from despair. Even before he'd steeped himself in the classics, he was busy constructing the inner narrative of his life, the transitions and motifs that would make of it something other than a simple, trite tragedy, complete with the simple, hard-working parents, and the chance at bettering himself, as they then said. "Bettering himself." Well, that's exactly what he'd done, and was it his fault, what happened? He hadn't meant to hurt the girl for Christ's sake. At most, he'd meant to scare her, and only because she was acting crazy—another crazy Negro woman who wanted more than he could give. Screaming and hollering that she was going to go straight to his wife. He'd never been so enraged. He still doesn't know exactly how she'd ended up dead at the bottom of the stairs.

"What was it, Mr. Wilbert? You got yourself involved in

drugs?"

"No."

"Because it ain't like we haven't got enough of those around here," she continues, shaking her head and making her black curls gleam under the fluorescent lighting. "We got all manner of 'em. But you want to know the truth? The truth is that there ain't a single being alive, ain't one, who hasn't sinned."

"That's what they say."

"And want to know something else? When you go back to Washington? Jesus gon be flying on that plane with you, sitting right next to you, because if you don't repent now, while you still here, you gon have to repent later, because, like I say, there ain't nowhere that Jesus doesn't go, and nothing that he don't see. Because he Jesus, you see? He Jesus. He God."

"Is he now?" Only he hadn't meant to say it out loud. Or maybe he had. He can't tell. In any event, the words are out of his mouth. Which meant that, at the very least, he's in for a full sermon, and at the worst, he's going to be subjected to the entire damn choir. The choir and congregation, both.

"Hell," he says.

Miss Beatrice just looks at him for a moment, looking at him as if she's looking for something *in* him, but then shakes her head, making Wilbert think, perhaps—could it be?—that he's been spared. Poor Miss Beatrice. She really is a sweet old thing. But like everyone else at Hope House, she's racing to her grave without ever having stopped to learn where she's been.

"And hell is where you going, too," Miss Beatrice hisses at him, her entire face changing from wide-open sweetness to ugly vengefulness, her eyes squinting behind her glasses, her small square teeth yellow, with badly receded gums, "unless you beg your Maker to forgive you for what you done!"

"And what," Wilbert says after a while, "is that?"

"You know what you did!"

"It was an accident," he finally says. "And anyway, I repaid my debt to society."

"Accident, huh?" And now he looks up and sees, of all people, his repulsive neighbor, Donny, slouching against the door frame in an LSU T-shirt and very short shorts. Truly, a more repulsive man would be hard to find, and Donny adds physical repulsiveness—the long stringy blond hair, the pock-marked face, the caved-in chest, and the tattoos—to a kind of rank presence that's as palpable as the smell of vomit. "Repaid your debt, huh?"

"This is none of your concern."

"Well, it ain't might not be, but y'all is yelling, and I can hear you clear as day. Everyone can hear you. Y'all sound like, well, I don't know what."

"We'll endeavor to keep it down," Wilbert says.

"Fine then." But Donny doesn't move. Instead, he leans in closer, and says, "All right? I know it ain't any of my damn business? But I got to say, Miss Beatrice, she's right. I mean, I know I ain't no paragon of anything you might be calling impressive, and seeing everything, you might even say I had made a mistake or two in my life." He pauses here, as if readying himself to parse Homer. "But the truth of it is?

You in this with everyone else. I mean, hell, I done some pretty rotten things in my time too, bro. And where'd it get me? Same place as it got you. Here." If, by "here," Donny meant Hope House, then Wilbert isn't aware of it, because he could have sworn that the "here" in Donny's "here" was the place of total collapse.

He feels funny, tight and tingly, as if maybe Beatrice and Donny had summonsed death to his bedside. A wave of nausea engulfs him, pain sears his chest, and sweat breaks out on his forehead. He winces, wiping away a sudden, strange tear. Could he be having a heart attack? But a few moments later, the strangulation eases, and he realizes that it's only indigestion—the chicken, apparently, having been a mistake after all. He lies back onto his pillows and closes his eyes, waiting for the attack to reside. As a new wave of indigestion hits him, he can feel Beatrice leaning in towards him. Her face held close, and her hand on top of his, she says: "Praise the Lord!"

He opens one eye to look at her.

"You done opened up your heart! I can see it," she says. "That's it, brother Wilbert. Go on. You can do it. I'm with you. You ready now! Just ask Him. Ask Him, and be saved."

LIKE A SISTER

Loretta is talking, talking, talking—the fact of the matter is, her mind is slipping some, and if she doesn't talk, well, then, she may well just forget what it was she was meaning to say. This time she's with that white girl. The white girl who takes her places. "What did you say your name is again?" she asks the white girl, who tells her. Oh yeah. They're driving. The white girl isn't such a great driver though: she drives like an old lady, slow, and Loretta wants to go fast! She wants to go so fast that her hair will fly right off her head! It's boring, here in the car. Boring with the white girl old-lady driver. Where are they going again? She asks the white girl.

"To Walgreen's. You wanted to buy some things."

"What things?"

"I don't know. Toothpaste? Shampoo?"

"Oh. Oh yeah. That's right."

What else? Because something is clouding her mind. She thinks and thinks, because she knows that somewhere, deep under the layers of her brain and the haze of her memories, there's something she's not remembering, and then she remembers after all: it's her brother, Bunny. Bunny is sick. He's so sick he's going to die! That's what the other white lady, the one at the place where she's been living, told her. "We need to prepare you, Loretta. Your brother isn't doing so well." Her brother. Did she have a brother? More like a sister.

"Bunny," she says.

"What about Bunny?"

"He different."

"I've noticed."

"He dresses up."

"Uh-huh."

"In ladies' clothes. Makeup. Shoes. Lord have mercy. What I gon to tell Mamma about him?"

"Your mother doesn't know?"

"Lord have mercy."

There's another thing too. She's hungry, that's what it is. She has gum though. A whole pack, right here in her pocketbook. She takes two pieces out. Juicy Fruit. Her favorite.

"Want one?"

"No thank you."

"What's the matter with you? Don't like gum?"

"Actually, not really."

Well, what do you know about that? Some folks be downright crazy, and some folks be downright mean. This one, she reckons—this white girl who is white and therefore doesn't know shit about shit about being black—she's a little of both. But not really, because, really, Loretta loves her. She loves everyone is the truth.

"I love you," she says.

"I love you too."

Well, there you go and doesn't it just go to show you? Loretta is so happy that she can feel the happiness as a tide of warmth spreading in her heart. That's Jesus in there. Because Jesus is love and love is God and she can feel Both of Them in her heart and this white girl is a good Christian. Taking her to the drug store, just because, and isn't that something, the way people can be so goddamned nice? Nothing in it for her, either: no money, no shit, no sugar, no nothing. But the good feeling turns cold again because all of a sudden she remembers what it is that she's worried about: she remembers her brother, Bunny, who dresses in women's clothes, puts on women's shoes and women's under-things and perfume and makeup and wigs and everything. When Bunny dresses up he's prettier than she is and men try to make it with him because they think he's a woman. She knew about it from long ago too because when they were coming up together she'd find things missing from her drawer, panties and bras, even a box of Tampax once, and then she found him prancing in front of the mirror, and he told her that if she ever told anyone he'd kill her dead.   Then he cried and said he didn't mean it but she swore anyway, swearing that she'd never tell anyone anything about it. He was already a big boy by then, too, almost six feet tall, broad and strong, with armpit hair you could see and little bristly bumps on his face where his beard was coming in, and here he was, stuffing her bras with Kleenex and squeezing his big male parts into her pink panties. But it's not even that that bothers her, because she's been knowing all about it since she was just a girl herself. It's that other thing, why the both of them are living in the place together, now, after all these years. It's why they're there that's the problem. How that other white lady, the one who's in charge, blinks behind her glasses, blinking like she's trying to get the blue of her eyes to stay put and not run all over the place like melting ice, blinking and saying in her dry white voice: "You know your brother isn't well, don't you, Miss Loretta? You know he won't be with us much longer."

"You're lying."

"Oh Miss Loretta. I wish I were. I wish I were lying. But honey, it doesn't look good."

"He's a strange one, sure, I'll give you that. Probably putting his thing where it don't have no business being. That how he get sick, putting it where it don't belong. Don't even want to think of it. But that's just the way he is, always has been."

"Oh Loretta."

"Just don't be telling our mamma about none of that mess, hear?"

That's what made her sad.

They'd loved to do the jiggle-wiggle, which is what they'd called it, back then, but it was only dancing they were doing: the brother dressed up in wig and evening gown, the sister in regular day clothes, him in giant heels, and the both of them dancing, shaking it, playing records on the stereo. The Funk Brothers, the Temptations, Martha and the Vandellas. Damn. She hasn't danced like that in years.

"Mind if I turn the radio on?"

"Go ahead. But we're almost there."

"Where we going again?"

"Walgreen's. You need to buy a few things. Shampoo, stuff like that."

She turns the radio on but something dreadful and dull comes out, so she fiddles with the dial until it's something she likes, with a beat, the singer's words coming out high and fast so she can't understand the words but it doesn't matter because it's that kind of song.

It would be one thing, she thinks, if the girl would just sing along with her some, but white girls can be like that: snooty. It doesn't matter though, because when she gets going, like she's going now, she just opens up and just like that she's lost in the music, her lungs filled with the joy of song, her feet tap-tapping and her hands beating the rhythm on her thighs, and, praise Jesus, she's happy. She's got a place to live, doesn't she? A room? A bed? Food to eat? And there's that man, too, the white man, real creepy looking, who keeps making eyes at her, and if he doesn't have the hokey-pokey for her her name's not Loretta Dawson, no ma'am, not that she'd go near him, not even if he begged her, because, for one, she's done with all that, and, for two, he gives her the creeps, with that long hair and those tattoos, and it isn't that she minds white men, either. White men; black men. Not much difference, both of them wanting and needing her the same way. But this one is something else and anyway: they can't have sex anymore, not at Hope House, not unless they want to get thrown out, and that's just what Miss Lilly told her when she was caught with that other man in the bathroom only they weren't doing much of anything.

"Do you mind if I turn the radio down a little?"

"What's that?"

"Do you mind if I turn it down?"

"Do what you want to do, baby. Your car."

Oh well, because the song was coming to an end anyway and shit: she'd forgotten it again. She'd forgotten the bad thing. It was back there, somewhere, some bad thing that she has to remember because if she doesn't remember it, it's going to get worse.

She takes out a pack of cigarettes: four left. Which means she can have half a cigarette now and finish it off later and then have another half later in the day and by then maybe someone else will have bought some cigarettes and she can have one of theirs.

"I'd prefer if you waited," the white girl says.

"What you mean?"

"I'd prefer that you don't smoke in my car."

"You mean this here truck here? You don't want me to smoke."

"That's right."

"Then why don't you just say so?" Not that she's offended. It's no big deal. It's just funny, how some people get all ticklish about something as nothing as a cigarette. Putting the cigarette back in the pack and the pack back in her purse, she says:

"You want to know how come I still smoke?"

"Sure."

"I ain't told you before?"

"I don't think so."

"See," she says, spreading her palms wide. Her hands are big in front of her: she's always had big hands. Even as a child she had big hands. "What it was was that, first, I got out of St. Gabriel's."

"I didn't know you were in St. Gabriel's."

But she was: sent down to the women's prison and had to work in the laundry and then had to work in the fields like a slave in the olden times and then back to the laundry and damn if it wasn't boring in there, and all because she took a shot at her husband, that no-good motherfucking motherfuck carrying on with her own aunt, found the two of them in the bed and didn't think twice about it, she grabbed the pistol they kept behind the flour and the sugar, way in back so no one would find it, and marched right into that bedroom—and it was her own damn bedroom, too, her own damn bed that she had made that morning before she'd gone to work—and took a shot, aiming at his head. She missed though and had to shoot again. Blood spurt out everywhere and her auntie jumped out of the bed with her little titties wiggling and her scrawny behind no bigger than a child's and she must have been the one to call 911, because even before Loretta had had a chance to clean up some of the blood, the house was filled with police, with firemen, sirens blaring, lights going criss-cross through the darkened windows. And the motherfucker wasn't even hurt bad: spent a week in the hospital and then went straight home, but by then Loretta herself was locked up at the city jail.

"Damn," she says now. "Yeah. And let me tell you something about St. Gabriel's. You don't want to do time there. Hear?"

"I'll keep that in mind."

"Place is nasty. But me, I get out for good behavior, only when I get out, where I gon live? My husband gone and divorced me and my kids are grown and they don't live nowhere near here anyway. So I move in with my mamma, and got me a job. A good job too. At the dry cleaning plant." Only she's forgotten what she was going to say. "Mind if I have me a smoke?"

"Actually—we're almost there. Can you wait?"

She looks at her hands again, thinking how nice it would be to have a cigarette between her fingers, and just like that, she remembers again: "So I was working. And every evening, when I get home from work, I go to the refrigerator and get out a nice cold beer. Then I lay out my stuff—first my cocaine. Then the beer. And I got my cigarettes for last. So I do like I always do, and I'm at the table, and I've got my cocaine right in front of me here, and my beer right in front of me there, and my cigarettes for later."

"We're here."

And damn it if she ain't right. The car has come to a stop in front of Walgreen's.

"I need me all kinds of things," Loretta says.

"Well then, let's go in."

Crest, Colgate, Aim, Aquafresh, Pepsodent, Arm & Hammer—only she doesn't need no toothpaste and doesn't understand why the girl is standing next to her urging her to make up her mind. Didn't someone back at the place make a list for her? She fishes into her purse, finds her cigarettes, and pulls them out, but the girl tells her she can't smoke in the Walgreen's so she stuffs the pack back inside.

"I know that."

She'd like one, though. Just one, or even just a few draws off one, just enough to calm her nerves so she can remember what it is she keeps forgetting. But now what's this? Her fingers have alighted on a piece of paper. Pulling it out, she reads:

Toothbrush

Soap

Panty liners

But everything is so beautiful, so dazzling, so colorful: and that music? How do they expect her to just stop everything and choose a toothbrush when the array is so intoxicating and the music—it's old school Michael—so insistent? Oh, she just wants to do the jiggle-wiggle, is what she wants to do, like she and Bunny used to do, back home, when they were teenagers, because with Bunny, she knew she could let loose, really be herself, really let go and go wild and no nigger would call her a whore and her mother wouldn't give her a lecture and the teachers wouldn't ask her if she'd always been slow and no one would say a damn thing and that was because when she was with her brother-sister, her secret was safe and his was too, and it was only just the two of them, Loretta with her big behind twitching like she wanted some even though all she wanted was to dance, and Bunny with

his wig and his perfume and all manner of women's under
pants and hose and perfume and eye-shadow on. And then
he'd press her to his large soft chest, and it was just like being pressed up onto her mamma's bosom, only not, because
Bunny was huge, well over six feet, and built massively, with
a broad chest and broad shoulders, a thick neck, and large,
strong hands.

"Oh yeah, oh yeah, oh yeah, oh yeah," he'd sing along,
coming in on backup.

In the candy aisle there were beautiful jellies shaped like
worms and bears and fish and they were orange and red and
yellow and white and green, green like the greenest green
there ever could be, and dark chocolates wrapped in silver
and gold papers, and enormous swirling lollypops. On the
other side of the store the lipsticks were even more beautiful, red and more red and dark red and pink-red and purple-
red all in black and red cases and glimmering and shimmering there in the light.

"Do you want me to help you find your things?"

"What's that?"

"Your things? Mind if I look at your list?"

"Help yourself, baby."

"Let's get you a toothbrush, okay? Soft okay? Because my
dentist always tells me to use a soft toothbrush. Better for
the gums."

"Sure."

"And what kind of soap do you like? Antibacterial
okay?"

"I like that real soft kind. Soft and white, like butter."

"This one?" She holds up a box with three soaps inside. "Is this the one you mean?"

"Yeah, that it."

The music's changed now. It's the Four Tops.

Baby, I need your lovin'....

"Mind if I have me a smoke?"

"You've got to wait until we're back at Hope House."

"That right? Well, okay."

But there's something else on her mind, and she remembers what it is: it's the story of the cigarettes. She says: "So it was Jesus himself who told me I could smoke cigarettes."

"Really?"

"Yeah. Because with those other things I didn't want them anymore. But with cigarettes, I never heard a word."

"What do you know?"

It was true, too: she was sitting at the table in her mother's kitchen, just like she did every night after work, and she'd laid everything out in front of her, all nice, all easy-like. Then she reached for her cocaine. But Jesus said: "No, Lo, no," and he took the taste for it right out of her mouth. Then she reached for her beer, and again she heard the voice of her Savior speaking right into her ear, right down into it so she could feel His breath inside her body, and again he was saying, "No, Lo, no my love," and she had no more interest in drinking that beer than she had in drinking a bucket of dirty mop water. Then she reached for her cigarettes but Jesus didn't say anything and even when she lit up He stayed quiet and right then and there she knew that she had His permission to keep smoking.

They're back in the car, heading down the highway, all manner of cars passing them, because the girl, she was real nice, but she wasn't much of a driver. Drove like an old lady. Stuck to the far right lane.

"You know my brother?"

"I do."

"Name Bunny? His real name be Lucas.   But now he Bunny."

"That's the one."

"He ain't right."

"Oh?"

"You know he likes to dress up in lady clothes?"

"I do."

"You do?"

"I do."

"You ain't gon tell no one, though, is you?"

"I promise."

"Because they don't let him dress up like that no more. Just pajamas."

"No problem."

It was true: Bunny didn't dress up any more, not now that he was sick and had to be taken care of, but only in regular clothes, sweat shirts and jeans and like that, or, when he couldn't get out of the bed at all, in clean men's pajamas, with socks if his feet were cold. The car is humming now but she doesn't like it, all this humming quiet, when she wants music—she wants to dance! Only she can't dance because, for one, she's in the car, and also, something's wrong, only no one will tell her what it is.

"He's sick, you know that?"

"I've seen him. He doesn't look well."

"He's real sick. He's just so sick."

"That's a shame."

"They say he gon die."

"Who said that?"

"That's what they say. They keep telling me that. But they wrong."

She flips on the radio again and again out comes all kinds of things that she doesn't much care for, so she has to go hunting around again until she alights on WFMF 102.5 all-hits-all-the-time only they're playing something she doesn't know so well so she can't sing along. She can't sing anyway, though, and that's the truth, because suddenly she's just so sad, so sad and downcast, she feels like crying. And it's all because of her sister-brother, Bunny, and how he likes to put on ladies' things. Puts his own thing inside of places it don't belong too which is how he got sick, putting it all kinds of places, and now he's dying. That's what they say, anyway. But they don't know Jesus and they don't have faith and isn't it God who decides who shall live and who shall die and not no white lady with little wispy eyelashes and eyes so watery blue that they look like they're made of skim milk?

"Here we are," the girl is saying, swinging the car around. "Door to door service."

"You're a good Christian, child," Loretta says. "You really is."

Back inside she looks for her brother but he's not in his

usual place, in his wheelchair, in the front room, where he likes to watch TV. Because the thing of it is that he doesn't much like to watch TV alone, in his room, all by himself. Which is why the ladies always be making a fuss over him and cleaning him up, putting him in clean pajamas and a robe and slippers and wheeling him out to the front room where, even if he's the only one out there watching TV, he won't be alone. But he ain't there. Instead, she finds that white boy with the tattoos flipping through the channels, his hairy legs jiggling like they're filled with bugs.

She goes to his room, but he isn't there either. She knocks on the door to his bathroom: nope. She goes down the hall to her own room, thinking that maybe he's waiting for her there. But the room is as she'd left it, messy and empty at the same time, the bed only partly made, and her dirty clothes in the corner where she'd left them when the girl had come to say that she could take her out if she wanted, and for some reason, all her other clothes are out and on her bed, because she must have gone and run out on them too. Just in case she takes a peak into Alvin's room just because Alvin sometimes has all kind of people in there with him, but a new person has moved into Alvin's room and he's asleep, snoring. Where's her brother? Then she remembers that sometimes they'll take him straight into Miss Lilly's office, or maybe he's having a bath? One of those special baths that the ladies who take care of everyone give him sometimes, in the big bathtub in the special bathtub room where they can lift you in and out of the water like a big baby. She's sure that must be it, especially as seeing that

Bunny had been complaining about how his whole body be aching him, and there's nothing like a nice hot bath when you feel like everything's hurting...but he's not there either and damn if she doesn't need a smoke because if Bunny has gone and died on her while she's been out shopping for pretty things she'll die on the spot, just cry and cry until she herself is dead, because Bunny is Bunny, and ain't no one else like him, her own brother who's also her sister.

She marches back to her room, retrieves her cigarettes from her purse—taking the whole pack, and not just the one cigarette she was going to smoke half of—and heads back in the other direction to the smoking porch. She's fuming now, twitchy with fear, angry at herself for leaving, even angrier at the white girl for taking her, angry at Miss Lilly for saying that he was going to die because if you say it it makes it that much more real, that much more like permission for Jesus to take you. She's so angry that she nearly trips over Veronica's wheelchair, so angry that when Veronica cries out in fear, all she can do is mutter at her about being in her way. When she pushes open the door, though, she sees him: her brother, Bunny, wearing her favorite dress, red with black buttons, his feet in a pair of her shoes, her favorite gold hoop clip-on earrings on his ears, and his lips covered with red lipstick. The only thing that's missing is a wig but he's gone and put some scarves over his head so he looks a little bit like a gypsy.

"Bunny!" she says.

"Lo!"

Even in his wheelchair, he's looking fine. He's looking better than fine. He's looking downright beautiful.

BLOOD INTO BUTTERFLIES

After Alvin died, Donny was the only white guy but a couple of days ago Charles moved in and now there are two of them, two white guys, there among all those niggers and nigger loving crack whores. There used to be another white guy, but that was back before, back when Donny first moved in and didn't know his ass from a hole in the ground, that's how sick he was, but then his mind cleared, and then the other white guy got sick and died, and Donny was the only one left. Which is what he's trying to explain to the new white guy. Trying to give him the lay of the land, telling him that he, Donny, had been the only white guy for maybe three, four months, because that other fellow—Alvin was his name—upped and died, which is what you get, he supposes, for getting fucked up the asshole. Telling him that some of the older residents still talk about Alvin, saying that he's in the arms of Jesus up there in heaven, which pisses Donny off, because even if there were a Jesus up there in heaven, why would Alvin be with him, after all his years of living like the faggot he was? Even so, Donny can't get all that worked up about it. Because now that he's sick—and fuck him if he isn't going to die too—Donny sees things differently than before. Like: he loves his mother. Actually, he's always loved his mother. Lets her know it, too. A better example: he doesn't hate fags. Maybe once upon a time, when he was a wild crazy pussy-monger, he hated fags, but why should he now? They're people just like everyone else, aren't they? Plus he doesn't say "nigger" anymore. Not ever. Even though the niggers call each other nigger-this and nigger-that all the time, and even sometimes call him nigger. As in: hey white boy, hey nigger, yeah you, you wan be seeing me? After all, he's not stupid. He knows as well as anyone that the only people who still say nigger are either ignorant low-life black niggers themselves or the kind of redneck trailer trash who fuck their own daughters. He doesn't hate niggers anyway. Now, the truth of the matter is that he never did hate niggers—how could you in Louisiana where there were so many of them that they were practically swinging in the trees? But he not only doesn't hate niggers, he doesn't even hate homo butt-fucking niggers, even homo butt-fucking niggers who drive SUVs and talk like they're the fucking Queen of England. That's how much he's changed.

They're sitting on two rickety chairs on the back porch, smoking and listening to the radio. Donny has it tuned to a country music station, but the new guy, Charles, doesn't seem to notice one way or the other. Charles doesn't seem to notice much, though, no matter what. Just sits there, gazing out at nothing, nodding only once in a while, but not so much in response to anything that Donny or anyone else says, but more like he's reminding himself not to fall asleep.

His light blue hazy eyes look like they've been rinsed in milk.

"First I thought, you know, that it would be wall-to-wall fairies here, you know, people who go around like this." Demonstrating, Donny raises his right arm, letting his hand go limp at the wrist.

"Uh huh," the new guy says, but there's no expression in his voice. Who knows, maybe he's a fag too. Donny's not sure, because on the one hand, he's real quiet, like a regular guy, like a guy who does it with women, but on the other, his hair is cut close, and carefully, as if maybe he'd just gone to the hairdresser. His hands are clean, too. Clean, with clean, rounded fingernails. Well, one thing he does know is that if it turns out that he is a fag, at least he'll know not to go after Donny, that Donny's not made that way, that he'd in fact kill anyone who tried anything funny on him. Because he may be weak, and he may be sick—he may even be dying—but he ain't no fag hoping to be fucked up the asshole in the middle of the night while everyone else is in bed, zonked out on pain-killers and dreaming of Jesus.

"Yeah," he continues. "When people hear that you're moving into a home for people with AIDS? That's the first thing they think of: fags. My own Ma was like that. 'You going to be living with a bunch of homosexuals?' she said. 'Is that where they're taking you?' Not that my ma has a problem with members of the American Society of Fairies. She's real open-minded. She just was worried that maybe I'd feel out of place. But then I get here and there ain't but one or two of them in the whole joint, and as I'm sure you've noticed, it ain't just men either. You get a look at some of these sorry-assed raggle-draggle women they got here? Young and old, don't matter, every last one of them is a sorry sight. But like I was saying: hardly anyone here's a homo. The only one we got now, leastaways as far as I can tell, is Wilbert. You seen Wilbert yet?"

Charles inhaled deeply and shook his head. He was looking intently at his right knee.

"You will," Donny says. "Room Two. Sitting up there like the queen of spades he is."

Charles puts his cigarette down.

"He's not a bad guy or nothing like that," Donny continues. "Just an old black fairy queen with all kinds of crazy ass ideas. Keeps mostly to himself." What he doesn't tell him is that Wilbert gets more attention than just about anyone else in the whole joint, even more than that loud-mouth crazy-talking Jerome did, even more than that sorry spectacle of a teenage crack-whore, Yolanda, did before she upped and died, leaving everyone feeling vaguely guilty, just shaking their heads and making those "tsk tsk" sounds that remind him of his grandmother, may she rest in peace. Wilbert is treated like a big pet, with all the staffers going in to check on him, and on Thursdays, when volunteer with the nice ass comes, she barely says hello to Donny, but goes straight to Wilbert's room, where she sits by his bed, talking with him. Then, when she leaves, she leans over and kisses him on the forehead. Donny wouldn't have believed it if he hadn't happened to see it for himself. And that girly coon does nothing but look up at her through his thick glasses and shake his head, all grateful.

And that's another thing: He's pretty sure that most of these niggers have never had it so good: room of their own, clean sheets, and best of all, three meals a day. All this, and all they have to do is be good girls and boys, mind their manners, stay away from pussy and drugs and shit. No wonder they're always going on and on about Jesus. He would too, if he'd gone from living the nigger life to coming here, where everything is clean and warm and there's a TV in every room, and the food ain't bad either. Priest coming by once a week to pray on them and nurses clucking over them and Suzette with her big boobs who comes in once, sometimes twice a week to drive them wherever they want to go: the Walmart; the discount cigarette store; their old auntie's up near the airport. Just listening to all their nigger stories as she drives them around in her mini-van. Shit! He'll give her some stories is what he'll do. He'll give her some stories and then some.

But all in all things aren't so bad, and he's comfortable. His room isn't any bigger than anyone else's room, but he keeps it spotless (he got that from his ma) and there's enough room in it for his paints and brushes and canvases. Because that's another thing about Donny, aside from his not hating anyone no more: he's discovered that he likes to paint. He made this discovery the first time he got out of the hospital, and he was sent home to his ma's to convalesce. One day, when he was watching TV, he came upon a show about painting, and on it, the old white woman who was the painter on the show was painting extremely real-looking flowers, which she then cut out and glued onto black velvet, making a kind of intricate, mysterious design. The old woman kept talking to the camera, because of course she wasn't in her own house just doing as she pleased, but sitting in front of a television crew, probably getting paid a lot to do it, too, and all she kept saying was: "I know what you're thinking. You think you need to go to art school to do this. But you don't. Just —that's it!—a dab of blue, a dab of pink. See how easy?" The tone of her voice as she prattled on about petals and stamens, about leaf veins and sun shine and the quality of light, mesmerized him. The next day he decided that he'd ask his Ma if she wouldn't mind going to the Walmart to buy him some paint and shit, and every day after that, he'd be sure to tune into "Caroline on Canvas," which was the name of the show.

So all in all, he thinks, it could be worse. He's got his easel set up in his room, and he has his art supplies: he's working on something he wants to give to his ma right now, a painting of butterflies flurrying around a delicate, Japanese-looking branch, and he figures that if she doesn't want it, why, hell, he'll give it to someone else, maybe even to one of the nurses or one of them raggle-draggle fat-butted nodding-in-and-out-of-it women, all of them talking together about how they don't know how they got the virus, talking about how their men done infected them, how they'd always lived clean, which was pure shit, and Donny knew it as well as anyone, having lived the life himself. Like that loud-mouthed cow, Loretta, the one always running her mouth, can't shut up, and when she ain't talking she eating? Just shoving it all in—potato chips and Coke and cracklings and just about anything else she can get her hands on, and her big fat lips all greasy all the time, like she's preparing herself to give a blow job. How many men did she do, Donny wonders, before she tested positive? A hundred? Hundred and fifty? God knows. Or Elizabeth, which was a pretty funny name for a dried-up prune-faced witch who must have been using from the time she sprouted breasts. Even the white chick, Lucy, with her big old eyes—how'd she get that wobble in her walk? How'd she get the shakes? Or big old Veronica, just lying up there in her bed for forever and forever, and babbling on and on: like you're meaning to tell him that these gals were saints?

Even so, he feels sorry for, and gets along with, every last one of them. He even hangs out with them from time to time, listening to their stories, laughing at their jokes, helping them out when they need help getting in and out of their wheelchairs or locating the remote control. They're all the same to him anyway. One big mass of sorry-assed humanity, just bent on fucking up. Well, he's the biggest fuck-up of all, and his mother ain't gonna like it one bit when he tanks, but if there's one thing he's always been, it's realistic.

"I ain't no kind of racist, you understand," he says. "I don't got no problem with any of these people here. I don't hate the homosexuals, either. I'm pretty much okay with everyone. Because as for me—back before I took sick, I was a long-haul trucker. Seen it all."

He waited for Charles to say something, or even offer an explanation of his own past, but Charles's eyes had moved from his right knee and now appeared to be studying the tips of his shoes.

"Yup. And in that business, well, you got to get along with everyone. Because you're going to be dealing with everyone. So even if, one day back when I was young and stupid, I hated homosexuals? That was just me being stupid. You get a little older, you see a little something of the world, you get to see how things are."

The two men sit there in silence for a while, sitting on the smoking deck just outside the lounge, listening to the sound of rain coming in from the direction of the river, and the hum of insects buzzing in the woods. One thing he's always liked about Louisiana, about being from Louisiana, is the rain: how, when it rains, the sky turns yellow and then greenish-gray and then, whoosh, there's all this wind and the birds start going crazy and then the rains come on, pounding through the woods and drumming on your roof. There are woods all around them here at Hope House, but not the real pretty kind, like the house where Donny grew up, about an hour west, past Port Allen. Here the woods are scrubby, filled with scrubby cheap wood: scrub-pines and underbrush and weeds and vines.

It's late February, still kind of cold and rainy, but not so cold as to put a chill on you.

"Rain supposed to be coming soon," he offers.

"Looks like it."

"You think?"

But the new guy doesn't seem to want to talk any more.

Now that he's in the death-house, he thinks a lot about

his life, specifically about what he'd do if he could do it all over again. Specifically, he thinks, he wouldn't have gone and married his second wife, because it was his second wife, Cindy, who had caused all the trouble. First off, he'd had to go and have kids with her, which was a mistake that he should have seen coming, seeing how she was no more fit to be a mother than a chicken was. But second off, he shouldn't have gone and married her in the first place, especially since it wasn't like he couldn't get it just about everywhere, even from women who were a whole lot better-looking than Cindy was, women who'd do just about anything just for the asking, and never wanted to talk afterwards, or discuss the future of their relationship, or any of that other hogwash that Cindy picked up from watching Oprah. And that was another thing: Oprah. What did Oprah know about shit? Big black bitch just rolling around in money, gassing off about everything under the sun, an expert on men even though she didn't have one, and, according to Cindy, an expert on him too. "You're in denial," Cindy had told him one night when he'd come home maybe half an hour later than he'd said he would, with a beer in his hand. "You have all the classic symptoms." Another time she told him that because he came from a dysfunctional family, he was stuck in an earlier developmental phase, whatever the fuck that meant. And that's what she did, just about every time they fought: she whipped out the Oprah shit. True, she never came right out and said, "Oprah says—" but she didn't have to. He knew what the source of both her grievances and her new vocabulary was. So one day he took a hammer and busted in the

TV. Which—given how expensive the thing was—was pretty stupid. But what was he supposed to do, with her going on and on about gender issues this and unhealed childhood wounding that?

She was a pretty girl, though, with her wide-spaced dark brown eyes, and her pert little bottom. Driven him crazy, is what she had done. And his ma had liked her too. Would he have married her again if he got to do it all over? Probably not, even though that would have meant no Donald Jr. or Rebecca Anne, who he barely knows anyhow, seeing as how, when Cindy left, she got a court-order from the judge down in Plaquemine saying that he couldn't come within one hundred yards of her house or she'd haul his ass back to court.

Another thing he thinks a lot about is whether, if he could do it all over again, he'd want to be born as himself—that is, as Donald Harold Spence, five feet eight, eyes of slate, as his first wife used to say—or maybe as someone else. For example, he wouldn't mind being Bruce Springsteen, who he loves, or even one of those big rich nigger rappers like Master P or Fifty Cent, just rolling around in money and cunt all day long. But the truth is, he knows better. He knows that it's not like, before you're born, you get to choose who or what you get to be. On the other hand, who knows? What if, before he was born, God had come on up to his soul—which would look a little white ball of light—and say, "Okay, then, you're about to be sent on down to earth to be born, but I got bad news: you can either be a fag or a nigger." Only of course God, being God, wouldn't say "nigger." He'd say, "African-American," or "black" or even "Negro" or "colored" like his grandmother used to say. Well, he had to admit that that would have been a tough one, because if he couldn't be him—which is to say a regular guy who'd made some mistakes along the way—he certainly wouldn't want to be some fairy either, no matter what. On the other hand, the way black people were today was something awful, and it didn't make him some latter-day member of the KKK to think so, either. First they squawk and holler about civil rights, but no sooner do they get them that all they can think of is moving into your neighborhood and taking your jobs away from you. And that's not even the worst of it, because at least the civil-rights niggers had jobs and houses, wives and kids and stuff. But all you had to do is take one drive through just about anywhere in North Baton Rouge to see that most niggers didn't have anything like the normal life that the civil rights people were all up in arms about back then, when Donny and everyone else he knew was just a kid, playing with GI Joes and dreaming about get-ting laid. Back then they talked about equality and justice and dignity, and all kinds of other high-flying notions, but so far as Donny can tell? Mainly niggers just liked living in their nigger slums, drinking nigger liquor, wearing nigger styles with their butt-cracks showing, and talking nigger-talk. That—and not lack of opportunity—is what landed most of the niggers at Hope House at Hope House, and that was the plain fact. On the other hand, there also were plenty of normal niggers, living normal lives—living almost exactly as if they were white. And this kind of nigger? They weren't just in Baton Rouge, but all over the fucking country, as he,

Donny, would know better than most people, given his former occupation. They lived in houses and apartments and wore suits and ties to work, and some of them drove big expensive cars and spoke French and God knows what else, and some of them married white women and had tan-colored kids, and some of them owned businesses and became judges and everything else under the sun too. And even if they weren't all rich or successful, there were plenty of normal working-Joe kinds of niggers too, like the gals who worked at Hope House, or the woman who used to come to help his grandmother once his grandmother got too old to look after herself, and needed help going to the toilet and bathing herself and shit. Plenty of them. Which meant that, when all was said and done, it wasn't much of a choice, was it? He'd say, "Okay God, you kind of put me on the spot, but go ahead and make me a nigger." Only of course he wouldn't say "nigger" because you didn't say "nigger," or even think "nigger," when you're talking to God.

The other thing he thinks about is what's going to happen to him after he dies. But he doesn't think he's going to the arms of Jesus, like all these niggers at Hope House are always going on about. He just thinks his mother is going to cry buckets and he personally is going to turn into nothingness. He'll turn into nothingness while his body parts get recycled as something else: his liver making a tree; his blood turning into butterflies.

So yeah: he might talk tough, and even do a pretty good version of the Southern redneck, right down to the tattoos on his upper arms and chest, but deep down, down where his soul is, he's an artist. His first wife, Della, knew that about him, how artistic he was. (She'd left him for a guy who sold insurance, anyway.) He used to make her things: necklaces that he'd make from sea-glass or bottle-tops; planters that he'd paint himself, by hand; once he even picked up an old chest of drawers that someone had thrown out in Massachusetts, and hauled it all the way back to Lutcher, where he'd sanded it down, repainted it, and lined the insides with pale blue paper the color of frost.

The thing about the new guy was: he spent an awful lot of time alone in his room. And it wasn't like he was that sick, either, that he'd have to be lying down all the time. In fact, he wasn't lying down. Mainly what he did was sit in his chair, either reading or watching TV. Just about everyone else, if they were feeling well enough to move around, watched TV in the common room, sitting back on the sofa just talking back to the TV set, the way niggers do. But not Charles: Charles sat in his room around the corner from Donny's, reading. Reading all kinds of crazy shit. Donny knew because one day when Charles went out for a doctor's appointment, he kind of stuck his head in the room, not for any bad reason, not to pry or sneak around, but just out of this kind of wistful curiosity, wanting to know what made the guy tick. Not ever having been much of a reader himself, he didn't know what to expect, but one thing he did know is that he sure hadn't expected what he found, which was big fat hardback books with titles like *The Embarrassment of Riches* and *Ludwig Wittgenstein: the Duty of Genius*. Which could only mean one thing: the guy was a fag after all.

After he found those books (and even peeked into one, which was a waste of time, given that he couldn't much understand a thing it said), he kind of steered clear of Charles for a while, figuring that he'd give the man space, let him get used to the way things went around here, and that by and by he'd try to make friends with him again, because even if he was a fag, he seemed like an all-right-enough kind of fellow, and at least Donny would have someone he could talk to, someone who hadn't spent his entire life shooting up and living the nigger life on the streets. In the meantime, he worked on his painting, turning out not just one painting (the one he wanted to give to his ma the next time she came to fetch him), but a whole slew of them—beautiful paintings, too, of birds and flowers and butterflies, and horses, as well. He's always liked horses. Paints their heads, their big big eyes. Tries to make their muzzles look all soft and warm; tries to get the smell of horse breath, of hay and sunshine and sweat, right into the paint, so that when you look at them, you could swear you're in a barn, and not just standing in front of a canvas with some color dabbed onto it.

He can do it for hours, too, just sitting by the window in his room, until his back begins to hurt, or his hands start to shake, or the smell of the paint begins to get to him, and he's overcome with nausea or fatigue or sheer, terrifying pain: the shooting pains that attack his gut and then swim around to torture his spine and ribs. But mainly he still does okay, and with all the paintings he's been doing, he's thinking that he's just going to go ahead and give one to everyone: one for his ma, of course, and the rest for everyone who wants one, including the gals who work here, and Suzette the volunteer, and every last one of them raggle-draggle women, and Father Ralph, and Charles, too. Something that they can hang on their walls other than the reminders to remember to sign out whenever you leave the building, and a list of regulations. True, depending on how long you've lived here, some of them have got all kinds of other things up in their rooms: family photographs, posters, Teddy bears and dressed-up plastic dollies sitting on the window ledge. But not a one of them has anything resembling what Donny would consider to be real art; not a one of them has something hand-made and so pretty it's almost magical, something made with love and care so that you can practically touch nature just by looking at it.

Only one who hadn't come by was Charles himself, which really burned Donny up, because, first off, he'd gone out of his way to be nice to Charles, even going so far as to tell him one day at breakfast that the next time his Ma came to pick him up and take him home for the weekend, he, Charles, could come too if he liked. "The house ain't much," he'd said, "but it's beautiful out there in the country, and my mother, she's a great cook, and now that my Pa has passed, well she gets kind of lonely out there. I know she'd be happy to have you." But Charles has merely nodded, as if taking in the suggestion that the sky, after all, is blue, and chewed his bacon.

"Been reading a lot?" he said.

Charles chewed slowly. "Uh-huh."

Charles wasn't the only person at Hope House who did

something other than watch TV and smoke cigarettes, though, and Donny wanted to tell him that. He wanted to say: I'm not like them, either—I'm not like them lazy complaining women, sitting around bored all day, talking back to Bob Barker on "The Price is Right" and rolling their eyes in that way they have, like maybe they're fixing to put a voodoo spell on you. He wanted to tell him that even though he'd fucked up so bad that he'd probably win the world championship of fuck-ups, he'd been raised up right, by parents who cared and taught him to stand tall and proud; he wanted to say that though he might not be Michelangelo, he, Donny, possessed a talent as true and deep and real as anyone's, that though on the outside he looked just like any old trailer trash, with his scruffy pony tail and tattooed arms, on the inside he wasn't that way at all.

Truth to tell, he's been painting so much that just about everyone in the joint has made mention of it, most of them coming by to watch him while he works, and remarking on how nice his paintings are, how much like life itself. "Yes indeed," Dianne, his favorite, said just yesterday when she came by to remind him to come and get his meds. "You sure do have the touch now, don't you?" Miss Lilly said much the same thing, and when greasy old Loretta came by, she rolled her eyes and smacked her lips like maybe she was going to try to eat some of the peaches that he was painting onto a peach tree. (He was more interested in rendering the blossoms just right, but had decided to paint a couple small peaches in, too, so people would know what they were looking at. He'd worked hard at getting the fuzz just right, with swirls of pink and dabs of creamy orange.) "Oooeeey," she'd said. "That sure enough is pretty!" Made him feel downright good, it did, to hear that, and it made him feel even better to think about how happy everyone would be when he told them that he was going to paint enough paintings for every single person at Hope House to have one of his own, and it wouldn't matter if you were a cock-sucking nigger street-walking kike, for all he cared. The paintings would be for every single person who wanted one.

He didn't tell anyone about his plan, though, because he wanted the excitement to build up some, with the other residents stopping by his room to admire his work, and even Wanda, who was the cleaning lady who barely ever said two words to anyone, saying how nice his paintings were. Even Suzette stopped by one day and said something about them before going off to hang out with Mr. Wilbert and let him stare at her chest, though why an old fag like Wilbert would be interested in Suzette's chest was something that Donny couldn't quite fathom.

By April Donny's room is filled with paintings: paintings stacked up against the wall and propped up against the bulletin board; paintings in his closet, and even a couple of real small ones tucked behind his bureau. His mother comes by almost every other week so she'd already had a chance to choose the one she wanted (delicate light-blue blossoms set against a deep lustrous black); as for the others, he didn't know if he should choose for them, or let them choose for themselves. He thought about it for a good long while and then finally decided that if he didn't choose for them, people might feel like it was some kind of competition, or like he was letting his favorites get first dibs. Mainly it wasn't any problem deciding who should get what, except when it came to Suzette and Charles. Suzette because she barely paid him any mind at all, but just came and went, driving off every day with her car-full of niggers bent on spending their Social Security checks on new CDs and strong-smelling hair products and Little Debbie chocolate cakes and all the other weird shit that black people liked, and Charles because Charles just didn't seem to care for Donny at all, and it didn't matter how careful he was to watch his language when he was around him; nor did it much matter, at least not in the eyes of Charles, that Donny spent time with even the laziest, fattest, and most low-down among the residents, laughing at their jokes and helping them with their shit—putting up some new wine-red curtains for that fat-assed Loretta, for example, and actually going so far as to sit by Veronica's bed and hold her hand while she babbled on about whatever the fuck she was babbling on about. Niggers and whores and fags and junkies and ex-cons, every one of them, but he sat there with them anyway, doing his best to be the kind of person he was meant to be, because Jesus or no Jesus, he was going to die too, and soon, and just in case Jesus was up there waiting for him, well, it never was too late for Jesus, now was it?

Just around the time he was painting the last of his flower paintings—having figured that he'd need ten or thereabouts for the residents, one for his mother, and another six for staff and volunteers, and whatever was left over he'd give to anyone else who wanted one—a new resident moved in. The day before, after lunch, Miss Lilly had gathered everyone together the way she does, to tell everyone that they were getting someone new, and, like always, she wouldn't tell them a thing about him, except that he wasn't a him but a her, that her name was LaShonda, and that she was coming directly from Earl K. Long. Which, Donny knew, meant that whoever the hell this LaShonda was, she was sure to be in sorry shape, because if the gal were even on half a leg, she'd be coming from her house or some kind of shelter or group program—any place other than Earl K. Earl K. could only mean one thing: that she was half gone already. Of course, new residents moved in, and old ones either moved out or got kicked out or died, all the time. So it wasn't any big thing. Just one more strung-out black crack whore shipped to Hope House to die.

But he was wrong. LaShonda showed up right when the caregivers were bringing in lunch. She came with her mother, an aunt or two, and a man who introduced himself as her brother, and who was carrying the bags. The main thing was this: crack-whore or no crack-whore, LaShonda was hot, with the kind of big old wide-hipped ass that black girls had if they hadn't had too many babies, a delicate little nose like a deer's, and a body that, Donny saw in a glance, was enough to make a grown man cry. She'd dressed like she was going out to the clubs, too, in tight-fitting blue jeans and a low-cut blouse, every finger covered with gold rings, and big gold hoops hanging off her earlobes. She couldn't have been over thirty, though with some of these black girls, with their dark thick skin that didn't wrinkle in the sun like white skin does, plus all that cocoa butter and all that other greasy shit that black women were always rubbing into their skin, it was hard to tell. Her mother and aunts and brother stood around the front room making a big fuss, introducing themselves, and telling everyone to take care of their baby girl, and then Miss Lilly showed them back to LaShonda's room, the girl's brother taking her bags, and the three women following.

"God Jesus," Donny said. "Talk about being wrong."

"What's that, Donny?" It was Dianne, his favorite, talking.

"It's just that—when I heard that the new resident was coming in from Earl K., well, I just kind of thought that she'd be real real sick, you know. I just didn't expect." He searched around for the right word. "That."

"Oh, I see," Dianne said, teasing. "Now you watch your manners, young man."

Donny thought about that for a moment or two, thinking about how he had changed so much that here he was, being teased by a big black woman who probably didn't make much more than minimum wage and said "acks" instead of "ask" and "gon" instead of "going to" and all other manner of lazy black talk, but that he not only didn't mind it, he welcomed it. A feeling of actual, bona-fide warmth pervaded his chest, spreading up around his shoulders and the base of his skull, and damn if it didn't feel good. He wouldn't have said nothing else, either, except that he wanted Dianne to tease him a little more, calling him "young man" and telling him to mind himself.

"Jesus God," he said. "Did you get a load of that ass?"

Dianne was still smiling, indulging him, he guessed, but some of the other women were looking at him as if he'd stepped in dog shit and was tracking it all across the floor. There was a moment of silence punctuated only by the sounds of the TV, which, as always, was on, but other than Dianne, no one was looking at him.

"Fuck," he said. "I know I'm an asshole."

"Yes, you are." It was Charles, gazing at him with his swirly light-blue eyes from over his plate of baked chicken and mashed potatoes.

"What'd you say?"

"I said that yes, you are an asshole. You're just about the biggest asshole I ever met." He said it like it was a known fact, something everyone knows, like the earth revolves around the sun, and not the other way around, or that China is a long way away.

"You telling me I'm an asshole."

"Looks like it."

The situation reminded him of before—before he took sick and his wife took off, taking off with their two kids, before she'd found herself a lawyer and slapped a couple of restraining orders on him, before he'd lost, first, his weight, and then his balance, and finally his strength, his ability to do the most basic things for himself, his sense of adventure and freedom, his erections, his innocence, his promise, his hope, and the small, untidy place he'd managed, despite everything, to carve out for himself in the world. Because back then, well, he was a crazy son-of-a-bitch, ready to fight anyone who so much as looked at him the wrong way. Got into some good ones, too, back in the day: a knife fight in a bar (that had left him with a permanent scar just under his left collarbone but nothing else); a fight with broken bottles and any other kind of shit that he found one night in an alley, when a bunch of skin-heads jumped him (he'd ended up in the hospital for that one, but not for long); and countless fist-fights, mainly in his last year of high school. And all kinds of other stuff too, with both men and women, who could be just as mean and low-down as men, and bit. But he wasn't like that now. He'd changed.

"I made you a painting," he said.

Two days later, Charles moved out, not telling anyone about his plans, not even telling Ms. Lilly, which Donny thought was pretty low-down, pretty inconsiderate and just plain rude, seeing as everything that Miss Lilly and all the rest of them had tried to do for him while he was here. He didn't have that much to pack, anyway: just his books and a few clothes. A friend came to pick him up, and just like that, he was gone. But he may as well have remained in his room, reading his books and not talking, for all the relief that Donny got.

"It wasn't your fault, what happened," Dianne said. "Some peoples just got to be mean no matter what. And the rest of us knows that you didn't mean nothing. That you were just saying what all the other mens were probably thinkin, anyway."

"If I was you," Loretta told him, rolling her eyes and

smacking her big greasy lips, "I'd a killed him. I'd a just gon right up to him and said, I gon kill you. He have no right talkin' to you like that."

"Some peoples just got to be like that," Dianne added, shaking her head. "They full of hate and they just gon go round makin' everyone round them feel just as bad and low down as they do. Well, you just never knows, do you? You just never knows." And she walked away slowly, shaking her head from side to side, her rubber-soled shoes making squeaking sounds.

But Donny knew. He knew that Charles had been right, and that he, Donny, was an asshole. He didn't mean to be an asshole, but there you had it. He was an asshole anyway, and just about the only person—or at least the only white person—who could stand him was his own mother, and truthfully even she had lost patience with him, which was why he was living at Hope House in the first place, and not at his Ma's: because his Ma could only take so much of him, and then she was ready to have her house back again, just the way she liked it, without having to cater to her fuck-up son, cooking and cleaning up after him, and, after he left, washing the bed linens and towels twice to make sure that all the HIV came out.

He stretched out on his bed, looking at the last of his paintings—this one of a hill filled with Live Oak trees covered with Spanish Moss. It was a bit of a departure for him, painting trees instead of leaves or blossoms, but he'd been intrigued by the challenge of making the Spanish Moss look real, all lacy and delicate and strange. After working on it for a full week, working to get that insubstantial, fleeting feeling in the delicate mossy greens, he was fairly satisfied with the results. He had intended to give the painting to Father Ralph, but now he's not so sure.

"I don't know," he said to the ceiling. He had to take a piss. But he felt funny, too, like maybe someone was gripping his heart. Then he had a peculiar thought: he wondered if maybe there was a special place reserved in heaven for assholes who hadn't really meant to be assholes, who had tried their best not to be assholes, but were assholes anyway. Because if Jesus really were God, and God was everywhere, and no one was born and no one died without Jesus God knowing about it, then maybe he'd get a chance to go to that place, clean up his act, and move on. With that thought in mind, he got up again, and padded into the bathroom. He still felt funny, with that squeezing, tight feeling in his chest, but the urge to piss was so strong that he couldn't wait for the feeling to pass.

Just as he reached for the door, his knees buckled under him, and the room turned white. He waited a while, hoping that the niggers were right and that Jesus was going to appear to him to take him on over to the other side, but he didn't see anything that so much as resembled Jesus. Instead what he saw was his own painting, which must have fallen with him, because instead of being suspended above him, on the easel, it appeared to be resting against the bed frame, on the floor. It was a good painting, too, almost as real as life, and filled with that special something that he'd put into the paint, that special something that he knew he hadn't learned, but had come to him whole, as a gift from God.

He stared at it for a while, waiting either to die or to be discovered by a member of the staff, because the truth was that he couldn't move, and the last thing he wanted was to be found dead on the floor lying in his own piss. He tried to call out, but the words had vanished, too. He couldn't say he was sorry to see them go, but it was still frustrating, just lying there, knowing you were going to die, and not even having a chance to empty your bladder first. But then his attention was distracted by something else, from something that seemed to be going on inside his painting. There, on the canvas, a whole parade of niggers, all of them dressed in white, started walking through the woods, just walking under the Live Oak trees with their delicate Spanish moss, as if maybe they was having a Mardi Gras parade. Behind the niggers were the fairies, who he knew were fairies because of the way they walked, all sashaying their hips around, and the way they wore their robes, kind of cinched in, like a girl's wedding gown, and after the fags were hordes of ex-cons, who he knew were ex-cons because each of their robes had a number stitched into the upper right corner of the chest, and then came the hookers, dressed, even in white, like hookers, with tall high-heeled hooker boots, and finally the regular sorry-assed fuck-ups, who were just about everyone else. He saw them all marching up the hill and then, when they got to the top, just ascending up and over the pine trees and Live Oaks, the honeysuckle and palmetto leaves, up and past the swarms of mosquitoes and the exhaust billowing out of the Exxon Mobile refinery. He looked and looked to see if maybe he'd see anyone he knew, but other than him-self—following along towards the back of the crowd, and dressed in gold—there was no one.

WAKING

Annie stands over Veronica, bathing her, as she has every morning for the past four years or so. Just bathing Veronica, and singing to her, singing to her as if she were a baby, which in some ways she is: a big black baby, laying up there on the bed, helpless, babbling. Babbling on like a baby. Not her fault, the way she babbles on: her mind doesn't work right, hasn't for a long time. There are moments, though, moments of clarity, when Veronica's blind eyes light up, and she sees, and knows, and understands. But those moments are happening less and less often, and it breaks her heart, but there's nothing she can do about it other than what she's doing. Some of them are like that: they get to you. There's just something about some of them—the last one, for Annie, was Jerome—but now there's Veronica, and Annie knows that when Veronica goes, she's going to leave another hole in her heart, along with the holes she already has.

Praise Jesus, Veronica would soon be taking her journey, soon be in the arms of God. Even so, Annie doesn't want her to go. Poor old thing is babbling on about her mother and her father, saying that her daddy's going to come and pick her up in his new Cadillac, when Annie knows full and well that Veronica's daddy had advanced diabetes and hasn't come to see her in more than a year, and wouldn't come to see her now, and might not even come to see her out of the world, it was just the way it was with some of these families, once their son or their daughter, their husband or their wife was at Hope House, it was so long, goodbye, later. Some of these ignoramuses still thought that you could catch the virus just by being in the same room with someone with AIDS, which is just such contemptuous nonsense that Annie has no words for it. After all, if you could get the virus simply by being in the same room, or touching the hand, of one of its victims, she and Dianne and everyone else who worked here would have been pushing up daisies years ago. Her own husband—she'd left him, but they were still married—had given her a hard time when she'd taken the job at Hope House, insisting that no woman of his was going to be working with those kind of people. What kind of people? she'd asked. You mean, sick people? No, he said, he meant those kind of people, white fairy pretty boys who flounced around like little girls, rolling their eyes and sashaying their hips. They gon make you sick, he said. That had been the first time that she'd seen, really seen, how angry he was. She'd left him seven years later, but by then her job at Hope House, which was steady, and had decent benefits, wasn't an issue. And also, by then the girls were grown up, one in college and one already in graduate school, studying to be an accountant, and she didn't need much on her own to get by. Just a roof over her head, a quite place to sleep, and a car that worked. Oh, but she'd had her a beautiful house, back when she'd still been living with Michael. It was his family home, way out in the country past Baker, surrounded by fields and trees, and in the morning, when she woke up, she could hear the birds singing, or the wind rustling in the branches, and sometimes she could even hear the sound of plants coming back to life after the stillness of the night, inclining their faces towards the sun. She'd always been like that—sensitive to nature. So sensitive that for as far back as she can remember, she's felt that all manner of living things, not just dogs and cats and horses, but also flowers and trees and grass, were not just alive, in the straight-forward, biological sense of the term, but rather, in constant communication with her, a relationship that she could choose to activate or not every time she stepped outside. But in old South Baton Rouge, where she'd grown up, there wasn't much in the way of nature. Not that it was a bad place to grow up: she'd liked it fine. But it was urban, and the most anyone had was a little scrap of a front yard, or a few geraniums in a pot. At Michael's house north of Baker she was surrounded by beautiful green, sweet-smelling things. The house itself was beautiful, too, built solid, of red-brick, with three nice bedrooms and two bathrooms and a modern kitchen with dark-oak cabinetry. Oh! She'd poured herself into that house, furnishing it with care, so that it shined like a showpiece. She'd left it all behind, anyhow, leaving not just the house, but the dining room set that she'd bought on sale at Olinde's, and the matching, powder-blue love-seat and sectional, and the framed paintings of the Louisiana woodlands that she loved so much, and everything else, too, taking with her only what she'd brought into the marriage: her clothing, family photographs, some dishes, a china tea pot, and two old quilts. The funny thing was that even after all those years of making a home, of lavishing her care and attention on the things in that home, once she made up her mind that her marriage was over, she walked out that door as if she'd merely been paying a social call.

"Baby, baby, baby," she sings. "Baby with your big old baby eyes."

"That's me," Veronica says.

"You sure got yourself a beautiful pair of big old eyes."

Four years ago, Veronica had been dumped on the steps of Hope House like she was a sack of dog food, and left to die. And that's what everyone had thought, too: that it would only be a month or two, and then she'd die, another body on the bed, another name attached to a cipher. Even Annie had thought so. But Veronica's still here, reminding Annie (who doesn't need reminding, but likes to be reminded anyhow) that no doctor, no matter how skillful, can really know how or when you'll die, and that's because doctors are only doctors, whereas God is great, all-knowing, all-seeing, everywhere and with everyone, mysterious in his grandeur, unknowable in his wisdom, and yet as close as your own breath.

But Veronica's not going to be here all that much longer. Annie knows it as surely as she knows her own deep fatigue. She can feel it coming off of Veronica, like a vapor, or like a bad smell that you can't quite identify. As she bathes her, her hands sense the breakdown of Veronica's internal organs, the great rumbling belly that no longer works, the female parts rendered useless, sexless, without meaning. Even Veronica, who is childlike in a million different ways, knows it, talking about her impending death as casually as if she were talking about the weather. I gon die soon. I ain't scared or nothing but you know I ain't gon be here for my next birthday. I still breathing? Thought maybe I'd already passed. Passed in my sleep. Only maybe I still here. Oh well. Maybe next time. She's a huge woman: huge, her flesh spilling over the sides of the mattress like pancake batter, her thighs the size of sofa cushions, her neck rolled with rings of fat. She's so heavy that they'd had to get a special hydraulic lift to get her out of the bed, so fat that she can't walk, but now she's too fat for a regular wheel chair, they have to order a special chair for her, but it hasn't come. Even so, Veronica's pretty, beautiful even, what with those almond-shaped eyes and delicate, flaring nostrils, her beautiful thick lashes, and that skin! Skin the color of caramel drops, smooth to the touch. Skin like a young girl's.

She yawns.

"You tired?" Annie says.

"I ain't tired. I just woke up."

"That's true."

"When's breakfast?"

"You already had your breakfast."

Last night, Annie had had a dream: she'd dreamt that she was pregnant, and so happy about it that she felt that she'd been transformed into something akin to pure joy. But she was confused too, not only because she was too old to have a baby, but also because she didn't know if she was physically capable of supporting a life growing inside her womb. She was further disturbed because, at her age—she was fifty in the dream, her real age—-she had neither the intention nor the desire to become a mother again. At the same time, she was secretly thrilled, secretly so happy that she wanted to scream. A new baby! A new baby! She wanted to cry it to the four corners of the earth. She'd woken up in the morning to find her stomach flat and her pillow, where she'd been lying on it, damp with tears. As she blinked, fragments of the dream returned to her, and then, just as quickly, skittered away, beyond memory and consciousness, out of reach. She'd gotten out of bed, stretching her arms overhead. She's always been a vivid dreamer, but this dream, she thought, couldn't have been important, or it would have remained with her.

But the dream comes skidding back to her now as she bathes Veronica, and she senses something that she didn't know when she was actually having the dream: that the dream was trying to tell her something after all, trying to tell her something important, that it was prophesying something to her, if only she could figure out what. She'd had dreams of that nature before—once, decades ago, when her sister died, and more recently when she dreamed that she was burying her wedding dress in a deep, dark hole. Sometimes, as in the case of the wedding dress dream, her dreams were transparent. But more often they weren't. More often they demanded that she delve into them, like a deep sea diver in search of scattered treasure on the ocean floor.

One way or another, Veronica's off again, babbling on about the man who, she claims, tried to come in through the window, to rape her, just like that other man had, that bad man, in the gymnasium, who raped her when she was still a girl, still in high school, and would Annie call the police, because she needed the police to come and get the bad man. Every now and then, as Veronica talks, Annie interjects, saying, "uh-huh," and "girl, you sure do talk," and other nonsense things, and sometimes, too, she has to stop Veronica, stop her from getting all carried away with her stories, scaring herself to death about bad men coming in through the window to rape her, and steal her baby, and punch her in the chest. She's heard this story before, about the man who raped Veronica in the gymnasium, only sometimes Veronica says that it was her own husband who raped her, and sometimes she says she was working at the school, she was a custodian at the school, and the man raped her, and other times she says that she was in high school, just a girl, and the bad man found her in the gym and hit her in the chest until she fell down and he did it to her. Sometimes when she tells the story she cries but today she's just telling it—and as best as Annie can make out she's telling the second story, the one when she was working on the janitorial staff—and she's about to interrupt her, to tell her that there are no bad men at Hope House, that she's safe, that the windows are locked, and that anyway there are people there to take care of her, when suddenly Veronica looks up (looking, as she does, into the darkness of her own blindness, into the flickering shadows inside her eyeballs) and says:

"Sing me a song."

"What do you want me to sing?"

"Sing me a church song."

"A church song, huh?"

"Sing 'Amazing Grace.'"

So Annie sings "Amazing Grace," and then "He's An On-Time God," and then she sings "How Do You Send Me?" She has a deep voice, powerful and sweet, and she likes to use it. Sometimes she thinks that she should sit herself down and write her own music, write the words and the tune, put her love for God right there on the page, let it out for all the world to hear, but somehow she's never quite gotten around to doing it, something's always stopped her, or, when she's tried, the words have somehow withered on the page, either that, or she's just been too tired. But she's never too tired to sing. At home, she sings to herself, praising the Lord, right there in her own living room, just singing and playing (she has a keyboard, though one day she'd like to get a real piano) and praising God. Now, as she bathes Veronica, she sways a little on her feet, back and forth, as if a wind were blowing her.

When she's finished, Veronica cocks her head the way she does when she gets an idea, and says: "Hey, Annie."

"What is it, Veronica?"

"Will you take me home with you? Let me come over to your house. I'll cook for you. I'm a real good cook. You like fried chicken?"

"Baby, you already home," Annie says. "We is your home."

"I home?"

"You at Hope House, baby. You with people who love you. You in Jesus' hands."

"That right?"

"And He ain't never gonna let you down."

A pause, and then Veronica looks up at her (or rather, she seemed to look up at her, all she could see was outlines, blurs of color, intimations of movement) and said, "Well, then. You have to spend the night with me."

"Where would I sleep, Veronica Jessup?"

"With me. In the bed."

"Ain't room for both of us, girl. There's hardly enough room for you."

"I'm fat."

"You ain't skinny."

"I got me a boyfriend anyway."

"I know that, darling," Annie says. "And his name is Jesus Christ."

But Annie hadn't always known that, which is to say: Annie hadn't always known Jesus. Not really. She hadn't even been much interested in Him. He came to her anyway, one night when she was laid up, her back sore from lifting too many old people (she'd had a job working at an old age home then), her mind sore from the pain of living. He flew in through the open window and stood in front of her, his legs braced apart, his arms open, so she could get a good long look at him. She liked the looks of him well enough, but that wasn't what tipped her off, because he looked just like an ordinary man—about five feet ten or so, with close-cropped hair and slightly big ears, wearing a Southern Jaguars sweatshirt, jeans, and scuffed-up running shoes—except that he was somewhat translucent, and he glowed. He had a white light coming off of him, but no wounds or scars or bloody palms—nothing at all, in fact, that made him look like he'd spent the past two thousand years or thereabouts hanging on a cross. He stood right there, just as easy as you please, kind of smiling a little, as if recollecting an especially funny joke, or a family picnic, or the first time he kissed a girl.

"Jesus?" she said.

"Yes, ma'am."

"You've come to take me away?"

"No ma'am. I've come to tell you that you need to get yourself down to the Good Shepherd Full Gospel church, on 9th and Main, in Central. Not too far from where you be staying. You know it?"

"Can't say I do."

"Well, you will," Jesus said, and the very next second, he was gone.

That was her second awakening, because it wasn't as if she hadn't been a Christian before. Which is to say: she'd always believed that Jesus was her personal savior, and she'd always been a church-goer too. That's how she'd been raised. But there had been mysteries along the way, and pain, too, which was followed, each time, by a glimmer of something pure and sweet like the finest perfume. The worst was when her sister—her only sister, whom she loved more than anything or anyone else on earth—got her first car, and the next thing you know, she's driven it through the guard rail on I-10 somewhere near Gonzales, just lost control of the wheel, and that was it. She was gone. Annie was fifteen. But the weird thing was that she'd known about it all along, known about her sister's death as if she'd already seen, already memorized, the story of her sister's life, already seen that climactic last moment when her sister's new, used Honda Accord, red like she'd wanted, smashed into that guard rail, crushing her sister's spindly body against the wheel, and squeezing the life out of her in an agonizing second—a second during which her sister had time to think: I didn't even have a chance to say goodbye! And: damn I'm gonna die. Her sister not cheerful and willing and peaceful, enfolded in the arms of the angels, but terrified and outraged, her entire life becoming, in that second, an agonized gasping scream. Ten minutes before the police showed up at Annie's door, ten minutes before her mother collapsed, sobbing, on the sofa, and all the neighbors came over, forming a human covering around Annie's mother as she sobbed. Annie knew. She knew as clear as she knew the sound of rain, or the feel of her own breath. She just knew.

"Momma, it's going to be okay," she said.

And that night, she had a dream, only it was more like a waking vision than like a dream: there was a fire in her dream, and out of the fire flew a large white bird. She followed the bird as it glided higher and higher into the sky, and then disappeared, and when she woke up, she knew that her sister's soul had gone to God.

But she still wasn't a Christian. Not really. She still didn't know Him, or what He wanted from her, or how deep His love was for every living soul. Years had to pass. Years and years. Years when she was alive, but only in a surface, here-and-now, go-to-work, mind-your-manners kind of way. Years when all of life appeared to her to be like a movie, running on its track, flimsy and unalterable.

She'd been feeling sorry for herself, is the plain truth. Her back had been hurting her. Really, she was just a vessel of pain—pain in her body, pain in her heart, pain on her mind. Her mother never had recovered from her sister's death, and in recent years had become an old, old woman, old before her time, her face furrowed, her hair white, and the strength of her body—the strength that had once enabled her to raise five children, hold down a job and keep house—all but gone. She wanted to die, is what she wanted. Every time Annie visited her, that's what she said, and it was a burden, seeing her mother like that. Worse, her husband, who she'd known practically all her life, and who she used to chase around the backyard with water balloons while their little girls, watching, hooted and screamed, had gone bad. Said things that you shouldn't say to no person, not ever. It hurt her, deep inside, when he got mean like that. There was a chill wind between them.

But that's all behind her now. Now she lives in the Light, filled with the Light, singing His praises, having church all by herself on the days she couldn't get to church, because there are times when the spirit is in her so strong she can't not praise him, and the music flows through her like water, washing her clean.

* * *

It's a Friday, last day of the work week, and James is visiting Veronica, sitting in her chair, talking. He's brought her something, too. He's brought her flowers. Six bright yellow tulips in a jar next to Veronica's bed, and next to that, a bag of chocolate-covered nuts.

James works for the maintenance department, comes around once a week to change light bulbs and fix air conditioning units and make sure that the ice machine in the kitchen is working right. He's one of the good people. He's one of the people who understands. Don't even matter that he's white, because his heart, his heart is deep blue. She can see it, right through his shirt, right through his skin: a deep blue heart, beating.

But that doesn't stop Veronica from sensing her, from knowing that she's there, in the hallway, and calling out to her, calling her out by name—Annie! Annie! Annie!—because even though she can't see, she can hear you, she can hear how you walk, whether you're wearing rubber soles or hard soles, or if you're tired. But Annie doesn't have time for her, not this second, anyway. She has to go and attend to the new resident, a woman by the name of Frances who had lived at Hope House a couple of years back, but then went back on the streets. Now Frances has come back to die.

"Annie! Annie! Annie!"

"I can't be taking care of you all the time, Veronica Jessup," she says. "I'll be in to see you later. And anyway, you

214

got company." She stands in the doorway for a second, grinning at James. "You got your gentleman caller. And I see he brought you something too."

"What he bring me?"

"He bring you beautiful flowers, Veronica Jessup. Beautiful yellow flowers. They next to your bed."

"Annie! Annie!"

"What is it, Veronica?"

"I love you, Annie."

"I loves you too."

She knocks gently, then opens the door. Inside the deep gloom, Frances lies curled into a ball, her hands, like claws, bunched up under her chin, and her legs curled before her belly. Her cheekbones are razor blades; her breath is a toxic cloud.

Oh, she's seen them come and she's seen them go. For ten year already. Seen them come and seen them go. The ones who are all belligerent, wanting you to be their personal nurse maid, ordering you around, complaining all the time—the food is bland, their belly hurts, they don't want to take their meds, it make them sick to their stomach, they want to know why they can't have a little party in their rooms if they want to, this is still a free country, ain't it? The ones who don't even know they're sick. The young girls—more and more young girls coming in, girls still in their teens, should be in high school learning their American History and how to write an essay—and instead they're at Hope House, watching their bodies break down. The junkies—both those who want to live right, those who say, okay, Jesus, take me, I'm yours, and those who turn their backs on the Lord, just aren't ready for Him, would rather put poison in their veins than live in the embrace of God. The ones who lie around in the bed all day, refusing to get up, refusing to bathe, or straighten their own sheets, or put their clothes away properly in the bureau. The ones who don't have any clothes to put away, that's how poor they are, that's how strung out, and Suzette has to go out to the Walmart and buy them underwear and shirts and socks. The ones who look around and decide that Hope House isn't so bad, and make their beds, and are grateful for every day on earth, and sit around with you, talking about their kids, their mothers, their old aunt, praise Jesus, yes indeed. Then there are the ones who have been around the block once or twice, the returnees, like Frances, who already know the rules, who've already been in and out of treatment, but who love the street more than they love their own lives, finally coming back to Hope House all humble and quiet, knowing that they're going to die, not even caring just so long as there's someone with them at the end, just so long as Annie or Dianne will sit with them, holding their hand, reading from the Good Book, praying to Jesus. Only sometimes they're not all humble and quiet. Sometimes they're angrier than ever. But their anger, Annie knows, is only a mask for the deep well of fear that's opened up inside of them. The way she sees it, it's her job to pull that fear out of them, to teach them that it's never too late to hand it over to God, and that, no matter what, God is good. Once they understood that—once they really understood that, not with their minds, but with their guts and their sinews—they were able to pass quietly, and at peace.

Blood behind the eyes. Blood in the iris and the pupils.

Back then, the first time she was at Hope House, Frances was a sly one, all sneaky and wheedling. Wheedled the Tuesday volunteer to take her to the food bank, even though she knew damn well that the residents of Hope House weren't supposed to use the food bank, welfare card or no welfare card. Wheedled the other residents to give her cigarettes, loan her money, let her use their radios and CD players, because she didn't have one of her own. Then she left anyway. Left because she was doing things she had no business doing. Left to go back to the streets, even though she had two little kids in the care of her old mother. But now she's back, this time, according to Miss Lilly, leaving behind a new child, her third. A half-white, half-black little girl named Kenya, like the country in Africa.

"How you doing this morning, Frances?" Annie says as she steps into the chilled gloom of the room. Room Eight, caddy-corner across the hall from Seven, where Veronica has lived for the past three years, living in that bed of hers, her big pretty face gradually sinking into itself, and directly across the hall from Five, where a new girl, so young that it's just pitiful, doesn't even understand what it means that she's infected. So many young people coming in now. And now here's Frances, only thirty or so, but as childlike, and as helpless, as a toddler.

"Bad," she says.

"Sleep all right?"

"Can't sleep."

"Well, if you want to, you can take a nap later. But it's breakfast time now. Got to get up out of the bed."

"Ain't hungry."

"You say that now, but later, you're gonna be. Better to try to eat something than to go on an empty stomach. Especially with that medicine you got to take. So come on now. Get on up."

"Fuck you," she says.

Even though she'd expected it—the "fuck you" coming almost automatically, as if Frances had been programmed years earlier to say it at just this time and with the exact same intonation of disgusted resignation–Annie's angry. She's very angry. And when she gets very angry, she doesn't hold it in. No sir. If there was one thing that living with her husband had taught her, it was that holding something back that had to be said didn't do any one a lick of good.

"Never, never ever, talk to me like that," she says, approaching the bed with one hand raised in a gesture of openness and the other one tensed by her side. "Never. Do you understand?"

Frances shrugs.

"Now don't be like that with me." Her voice is as calm as water. "Because the way I see it? The way I see it is that you ought to be down on your hands and knees, thanking me, and thanking everyone else who works here, and thanking the people at the hospital who pay for this place, and thanking the government who pays for your medication, and most of all, thanking Jesus Christ who led you here, and that the last thing you want to be doing, now or ever, is disrespecting me. Are we clear?" She doesn't wait for an answer. "The way I see it? You've spent most of your life disrespecting yoself.

Abusing yoself. Pimping yoself. Poisoning yoself. But you come inside these walls, baby, and it over. Understand? It over. You go disrespecting me, or anyone else here at Hope House, and you back on your ass in the street, and if that's what you want, you can go and die in the gutter, howling for mercy like a dog. Is that what you want, Frances? Is it?"

She'd worked herself up into a nice little fury, working her broad chest until it heaved, and opening up her strong lungs and vocal chords until what came out sounded more like a sermon, or a hymn, than what was, in fact, a pretty standard-issue lecture, a fairly straight-forward talking-to. (Oh! She'd done it before! Countless times.)

"Is it?" she says. "Is that what you want? You want to die in the streets like an abandoned dog?" Frances doesn't say anything, but it doesn't matter. Annie hears the "no" as clearly as if Frances had shouted it from the rooftops.

That night, she has the dream again, only this time she's pregnant with twins. She wakes with the same swirl of conflicting emotions, blinking into the semi-darkness of dawn, and unable to locate where she is: in her childhood bed at home on South 11th Street? With Veronica, at Hope House? At home in Baker with her husband? Only if it's the latter, where is her husband? Until finally she wakes into everyday consciousness, and sees her wooden bureau with its display of framed family photographs on top, her work clothes laid out on the chair, the book she was reading last night before she fell asleep resting on her night-stand.

She has the dream the next night, too, and the next night after that, each time with its insistent lack of clarity, and its equally insistent clarity: the swelling belly, the tender breasts, the sense that she is about to give birth to no less than a miracle. And then, upon waking, she's filled with a disappointment so keen that it's like drowning. In real life, her pregnancies hadn't been particularly noteworthy one way or another: she'd neither been nauseated and tired, nor elated and glowing with expectation. It wasn't that she was indifferent to her unborn children, or her own looming motherhood, either. It was just that she felt prepared for the job, competent. Both girls had been born in the middle of the night, at the hospital, coming quickly once the pains came on, and weighing a perfect seven pounds even.

It's this basic competence of hers—her ability to quickly and efficiently cut through confusion and see her way to truth—that is, she knows, at the forefront of her personality. It is this trait, too, that allowed her to leave her husband without regret or rancor, and to have taken on the job at Hope House, with all its sorrow. Even her appearance, her face and her body, yield up her competence, for God had seen fit to give her strong legs and arms, and a broad, almost masculine body, along with a face that rarely shows much in the way of emotion while still conveying intelligence. Her eyes are small and her black hair, which once she'd worn long and wrapped around her head, is now cut as short as a man's. She keeps her fingernails cut short, too, because they're easier to care for that way, and because she doesn't want to inadvertently scratch one of the residents in her care. Yet she also dwells in another dimension, a reality that's just as real to her as the clocks on the wall and the endless rounds of laundry she does for residents too weak to do it for themselves. They exist within her, side-by-side.

It was a full week of dreaming that same dream night after night—a week during which she'd had two days off, and had gone to church, visited both her daughters, dropped in on her sister-in-law, paid her bills, read the newspaper, and set herself to trying to write a song in praise of Jesus (she hadn't gotten very far, but still)—before she finally came to understand what the dream meant. And once she understood what the dream meant, it was so clear to her that she slapped the side of her head like a character in a TV sitcom.

It was a dream about Veronica. The baby in her dream—the baby that she was tasked to give birth to—was no one but Veronica Jessup. The baby was in danger only because the mother, who was Annie herself, was confused about her role, uncertain as to whether or not she could once more give birth. But hadn't Jesus Himself guided her all of her days? And hadn't God Himself, in his goodness, given her the dream? It was a test of faith; nothing more, and nothing less. God was calling on her to call on Him; he was asking her to ask of Him. All she had to do was pray sincerely, from her heart. All she had to do was ask God to spare Veronica, and to return her to life. Because, after all, hadn't he brought Daniel out of the Lion's Den? And parted the Red Sea for the Children of Israel? Hadn't He turned water into wine? And appeared to Moses in the guise of a bush that burned and yet was not consumed? Veronica, she knew, would merely be a grace-note to all this, practically an after-thought. And no one other than Annie herself would know what had really happened.

"Baby girl," she says the next time she goes to visit Veronica. "Guess what?"

"What? I dead already?"

"No ma'am. You ain't dead. And I don't think God intends you to be dead, either. Not for a little while, anyhow."

"How you know that?"

"Let's just say I got a sense."

"You been praying on me?"

"Why you ask a question like that? You know you always in my prayers."

It's true, too: Annie never fails to pray for the well-being of the people whom God has put in her care, and lately, she's been praying doubly hard for Veronica. But now that she's been tasked by God to bring about a miracle—a miracle not made by Annie herself, but merely delivered by her, like a milkman delivering milk—she's been praying with even greater ferocity, greater abandonment, greater joy and passion. She prays aloud, in her own home, swaying and rocking, crying and singing, in postures of full supplication and of full openness, her face raised towards the heavens, her arms outstretched and reaching.

"Yeah, baby," she says. "You ain't going anywhere, at least not straight-aways. So you stop all that talk about dying, you hear me?"

"If you say so."

Truly, God works miracles, for no sooner had she left

Veronica's room than Gordon and Lucy were rounding the corner, looking just as sweet and goofy as could be, their expressions reminding her more than anything of the faces of her girls when they were little and trying to keep a secret.

"We got news. Want to know it?" Gordon said.

"What?"

"I'm clean. I swear to God, I'm clean as the day I was born. Gordon done took me down to his church, and well, it ain't Catholic or nothing, but I was washed clean. Jesus gone and filled me with something better than drugs. He gone and filled me with Him."

"That's right," Gordon says, a protective hand over her shoulder. "She's not just clean. She's clean clean."

"Yeah, because Miss Lilly say she was gonna throw me right out, and then Gordon say he cain't marry me 'less I pure."

"You getting married?'

"We aim to."

Their happiness was so powerful that Annie felt it on her skin like a warm spring mist. She had to wait for the miracle to happen though, because Jesus didn't perform miracles in human time, or to the tune of human desire. He acted when He was good and ready.

In the meantime, she does as she always does, serving the residents at Hope House as best she can, joking around with Gordon, consulting with Dianne, bathing Veronica, and making sure that Frances behaved herself, and took all her medication, and remembered to bathe. Poor thing. Fact of the matter is, once she'd had her little talking-to with her, Frances had become just as sweet and docile, as humble and willing, as could be. Just about every day, she and Frances would sit together, trading stories and laughing, and when she could—on those days when she wasn't too weak or too sick to sit up and get around—she even helped out a little, bringing treats for Veronica, sharing her cigarettes. As for the way she behaved towards Annie—all Annie could say was that Jesus was indeed good, that he'd turned Frances's heart, bringing her close to Him in preparation for her final journey. Now, when Annie knocked on her door to see how she was doing, Frances smiled and waved her in. Now, when Annie had a few spare minutes, and wanted to know if Frances needed anything, Frances would hold her hand, and tell her all about herself—telling her about her children, her childhood in Plaquemine, how she'd come to be so low, and how, as a girl growing up, she'd planned a future for herself as a teacher or a secretary or perhaps even a pilot (she used to love to gaze up at the skies and see the airplanes swooping over the bayous towards the airport). She was, she said, a complete failure.

Annie would argue with her, pointing out that though Frances had made all kinds of stupid decisions, disrespecting not only herself but the holy spark that God had implanted in her, she had now come to a place of wisdom and acceptance. "That's Jesus working through you," she said. "And ain't nothing sweeter than that."

"Amen," Frances said.

They grew so close that in May, not long after Veronica made thirty-eight and the staff hauled her out to the front room for birthday cake and ice cream, strapping her into a reclining chair because the special wheel chair they'd ordered for her still hadn't come, Frances told Annie that if she could do it all over again, she'd want God to have made Annie her mother.

"What are you talking about? Your mamma your mamma. Ain't got but one."

"That's true," Frances said. "But I just keep thinking that if maybe you'd been my mamma instead? Then maybe I wouldn't be here now. Then maybe I wouldn't be sick, and worrying about my kids, and just counting down the minutes until I die."

"Don't be talking like that," Annie said. "Your mamma did the best she could."

"That's true," Frances agreed. "But you know? My mamma was beaten-down. She could barely look after herself. Let all us kids run wild. And now I went and did the same thing. And my own children? I don't know what's going to become of them, especially my baby, my Kenya. The other two? The two older ones? Looks like their daddy going to be taking them. But I don't know what-all's going to happen to my baby, because mamma, well, she can't look after no one, and Kenya's daddy's in prison, and my cousin who keeping her now don't really want her, she just keeping her because she can't right not keep her, but it don't set right on my mind, my baby up at my cousin's, and no one really loving her right."

But Annie couldn't be spending too much of her energy worrying about Frances's kids, not when there were so many other folks to worry about. Veronica was getting sicker, wearing a diaper and unable to control her bladder, riddled with pain, and growing more and more confused. Annie kept praying, praying and praying as if the whole world were dependent on her prayers alone—as if the whole world were made of her prayers alone—but one day, when Annie showed up for work, Miss Lilly took her aside and told her that the night before, shortly after Annie had left for the day, Veronica had spiked a fever and had to be taken to the hospital, and that just this morning, at dawn, she'd passed away.

She is falling down a hole. Her head is filled with noise.

"I'm so sorry to have to tell you like this," Miss Lilly is saying, "and I would have called you at home to let you know, but it just happened so suddenly." Her voice trails off. Miss Lilly is one of those white women who looks so soft, it's almost as if they don't have bones in their bodies at all, but just a lot of soft white stuffing. She wears oversized plastic-framed glasses that exaggerate the size of her eyes. "But we all knew it was coming. It was just a matter of time, and, well, it's not like we haven't been through this before. But Veronica—well, she was just special."

It's as if she were hearing about her sister's death all over again, seeing it pass before her eyes as if she'd been there, only this time, she has work to do, duties to perform. Ieesha, in Room Six; Loretta, in Ten. Drugs to dispense. Meals to order. Fingernails and toenails. By the time Annie gets home she feels as if she'd just awoken from a surgery, only to discover that all her blood had been drained from her body. Or perhaps it isn't her blood that's been taken. Perhaps it's her heart, or her liver, or even her memory. "My baby!" she cries, falling on her knees on the kitchen floor. "My sweet sweet girl!"

There were so many different ways to die at Hope House, and in her years there, she has seen them all. The best were the ones who died quietly in their rooms, surrounded by family, or, in the absence of family, surrounded by the people who had cared for them in their suffering. Annie has lost count of the times that it was she—with Dianne or Miss Lilly—who had seen one or another resident out of the world, sitting by their beds, holding their poor limp hands, sponge-bathing their hot heads, murmuring words of strength and love and consolation. Those were the good ones, the peaceful ones, the ones where you knew, afterwards, that the person had gone on to a better place, was free of pain, and drifting to glory. (Annie could never bring herself to just up and leave the body after the life had departed from it, usually sitting for another hour or so, holding the body's hands, and praying.) Alvin had been like that, holding onto her hand until the end, when he'd gasped, opened his eyes, mouthed the words "I love you," and died. The worst were those who died in the hospital. Most of the time, when someone died in the hospital, you didn't even get to say goodbye to them, or if you did, it was already too late—the person was unconscious, hooked up to machines, or already so deeply retreated into himself that the person who you once knew and cared for may as well be a store mannequin. And then they died, usually by themselves, surrounded by other bodies hooked up to other machines, and attended to by strangers.

And now the deaths started coming: Donny died; Loretta died; Mr. Wilbert died; a cranky middle-aged homosexual named Larry—all of them, one after another, like falling dominoes. A new woman moved into Yolanda's room, a pretty young woman named LaShonda who didn't look the slightest bit sick, and she died too. A man named Archer moved in, did weed, got kicked out, and died on the streets. Father Ralph had been the one to break the news, crestfallen, as if even he had lost hope. The only one who still seems to be holding on is Frances, only Frances isn't doing well either, you had to be an idiot not to see it. Her eyes are huge in her face; what little hair she has left is plastered to her skull as if it had been glued on; her lips are perpetually chapped; and no matter how many times Annie gives her a sponge bath or brushes what's left of her hair (pulling it back into a tiny top-knot on her head) she smells bad, like rotting meat, or overripe garbage. Her children don't come to see her, but nearly every day, she cries out for them, saying that the first two have a father, but the little one: who will take care of her little one?

"My Kenya!" she cries. "My beautiful little girl!"

"Shh, shh, you've got to stop that fretting," Annie advises. "What you have to do? You have to give it over to God. He already knows what's in your heart and in your soul. He just waiting on you to put your trust in Him."

But even as she says the words—words that, one way or another, have crossed her lips nearly every day since becoming a Christian—she hears the emptiness of them, the hollowness, the vicious, cold lie. Because no matter how much and how often and how fervently she prays, they up and die anyway, just upping and dying, one after another, even as they cling onto life. Jesus. Where was Jesus now? What did He want of her? Why did He send her dreams? Was He testing her? Taunting her? At night, when she comes home, instead of praying to Jesus, she prays to Veronica, begging her, supplicating her, for mercy and forgiveness. She knows it's a sin: she knows that Veronica can't hear her, and that only God is God. But the God to whom she has given all her heart and all her soul, all her love and all her passion, has become a deaf-mute.

"Dear sweet girl," she says, directing her words to her living room ceiling. "I'm sorry. I'm sorry I let you die in the hospital. I'm sorry I wasn't with you." She half expects that Veronica will return her pleas, calling out to her as she had in life: Annie! Annie! When you gon come sit with me, Annie?

Praying like that all winter long, half to Veronica, and half to God. Praying and praying, with no reply.

One day in early June, when Annie passes Frances's door carrying linens and a pillow for yet another new resident, Frances calls out to her, calling with the ferocity of her former self, the person she'd been before she'd been redeemed: "Annie! I be needing you now, Annie! I know you out there. I can see you. I need to talk to you, and no it can't wait. Annie!"

"I'll be in in a minute, Frances. Just let me do what I got

to do and then I'll be in to see you."

"No! Now!"

As always, Frances is lying on her back under the covers, the shades drawn. The room is overheated, and even gloomier than usual. Unlike some of the other residents, Frances had never tried to make her room homey. Aside from three photographs of her three children, there is little in the room to indicate that it is occupied by a particular person with a particular personality. The television is on, and blaring, but Frances isn't watching it. Instead, she stares into the mid-distance, as if seeing something that only she has access to.

"Annie?"

"What you want, Frances?"

"I need to talk to you Annie."

"You know you can talk to me."

"No," she says, "I mean: I really needs to talk to you."

"Okay," Annie says, "What you want to talk about?"

Really, it's amazing to her, that she's able to carry on like this, dispensing comfort and advice, medicine and prayer, when she herself is merely an imitation of herself. But she does it anyway—and has been doing it—day in and day out, week after week, fooling everyone. Even Dianne hasn't noticed much of a change, and on the one or two occasions when she's cocked her head and said, "Anything bothering you, Annie?" she's been satisfied with Annie's explanation of being over-tired, or fighting off a cold.

"Come here," Frances says. Annie doesn't like being ordered around, not by anyone, but she does as she's told, taking a seat in the room's one chair.

"Okay, what you want to talk to me about? What's so important?"

"It's about my little girl," Frances says.

She dreams that night that she's in labor, a long, painful labor, the baby stuck. The head is stuck; and then it's the feet. There is blood everywhere and the sound of her own grunting and as she pushes and sweats and strains, shit and piss falling out of her onto the floor, there is so much mess in her, so much foul substance, but the baby is in there too, a little girl, and the baby needs to be born. When at last, around five in the morning, just before the alarm goes off, the baby emerges into the world, they hold her up before her, and Annie sees that she is perfect.

And it is in this way that Annie agrees to adopt Frances's youngest child, Kenya. The child calls her Mamma Annie, to distinguish her from her mother in heaven, Mamma Frances. She sits next to Annie on the sofa, while Annie reads to her, and runs around Annie's living room, pretending to be a lion. During the day she stays at the day-care at church, but every night, she's home, with Annie, and in the morning, she wakes her with a kiss. Ah, but God is good. Such joy He has given her! Such impossibly perfect joy!

About the Author

Jennifer Anne Moses is a writer and painter. Other books include *Food and Whine* and *Bagels and Grits: A Jew on the Bayou.* She lives with her husband, three children, and two mutts in Montclair, New Jersey.

Learn more at www.JenniferAnneMosesArts.com

Fomite

Burlington, Vermont

Fomite is a literary press whose authors and artists explore the human condition -- political, cultural, personal and historical -- in poetry and prose.

A fomite is a medium capable of transmitting infectious organisms from one individual to another.

"The activity of art is based on the capacity of people to be infected by the feelings of others." Tolstoy, *What is Art?*

AlphaBetaBestiario - Antonello Borra
Animals have always understood that mankind is not fully at home in the world. Bestiaries, hoping to teach, send out warnings. This one, of course, aims at doing the same.

Flight and Other Stories - Jay Boyer
In *Flight and Other Stories,* we're with the fattest woman on earth as she draws her last breaths and her soul ascends toward its final reward. We meet a divorcee who can fly for no more effort than flapping her arms. We follow a middle-aged butler whose love affair with a young woman leads him first to the mysteries of bondage, and then to the pleasures of malice. Story by story, we set foot into worlds so strange as to seem all but surreal, yet everything feels familiar, each moment rings true. And that's when we recognize we're in the hands of one of America's truly original talents.

Improvisational Arguments - Anna Faktorovich
Improvisational Arguments is written in free verse to capture the essence of modern problems and triumphs. The poems clearly relate short, frequently humorous and occasionally tragic, stories about travels to exotic and unusual places, fantastic realms, abnormal jobs, artistic innovations, political objections, and misadventures with love.

Fomite
Burlington, Vermont

Loisaida - Dan Chodorokoff

Catherine, a young anarchist estranged from her parents and squatting in an abandoned building on New York's Lower East Side is fighting with her boyfriend and conflicted about her work on an underground newspaper. After learning of a developer's plans to demolish a community garden, Catherine builds an alliance with a group of Puerto Rican community activists. Together they confront the confluence of politics, money, and real estate that rule Manhattan. All the while she learns important lessons from her great-grandmother's life in the Yiddish anarchist movement that flourished on the Lower East Side at the turn of the century. In this coming of age story, family saga, and tale of urban politics, Dan Chodorkoff explores the "principle of hope", and examines how memory and imagination inform social change.

Still Time - Michael Cocchiarale

Still Time is a collection of twenty-five short and shorter stories exploring tensions that arise in a variety of contemporary relationships: a young boy must deal with the wrath of his out-of-work father; a woman runs into a man twenty years after an awkward sexual encounter; a wife, unable to conceive, imagines her own murder, as well as the reaction of her emotionally distant husband; a soon-to-be tenured English professor tries to come to terms with her husband's shocking return to the religion of his youth; an assembly line worker, married for thirty years, discovers the surprising secret life of his recently hospitalized wife. Whether a few hundred or a few thousand words, these and other stories in the collection depict characters at moments of deep crisis. Some feel powerless, overwhelmed—unable to do much to change the course of their lives. Others rise to the occasion and, for better or for worse, say or do the thing that might transform them for good. Even in stories with the most troubling of endings, there remains the possibility of redemption. For each of the characters, there is still time.

Loosestrife - Greg Delanty

This book is a chronicle of complicity in our modern lives, a witnessing of war and the destruction of our planet. It is also an attempt to adjust the more destructive blueprint myths of our society. Often our cultural memory tells us to keep quiet about the aspects that are most challenging to our ethics, to forget the violations we feel and tremors that keep us distant and numb.

Fomite
Burlington, Vermont

Carts and Other Stories - Zdravka Evtimova

Roots and wings are the key words that best describe the short story collection, *Carts and Other Stories,* by Zdravka Evtimova. The book is emotionally multilayered and memorable because of its internal power, vitality and ability to touch both the heart and your mind. Within its pages, the reader discovers new perspectives true wealth, and learns to see the world with different eyes. The collection lives on the borders of different cultures. *Carts and Other Stories* will take the reader to wild and powerful Bulgarian mountains, to silver rains in Brussels, to German quiet winter streets and to wind bitten crags in Afghanistan. This book lives for those seeking to discover the beauty of the world around them, and will have them appreciating what they have — and perhaps what they have lost as well.

The Listener Aspires to the Condition of Music - Barry Goldensohn

"I know of no other selected poems that selects on one theme, but this one does, charting Goldensohn's career-long attraction to music's performance, consolations and its august, thrilling, scary and clownish charms. Does all art aspire to the condition of music as Pater claimed, exhaling in a swoon toward that one class act? Goldensohn is more aware than the late 19th century of the overtones of such breathing: his poems thoroughly round out those overtones in a poet's lifetime of listening."

John Peck, poet, editor, Fellow of the American Academy of Rome

When You Remember Deir Yassin - R.L Green

When You Remember Deir Yassin is a collection of poems by R. L. Green, an American Jewish writer, on the subject of the occupation and destruction of Palestine. Green comments: "Outspoken Jewish critics of Israeli crimes against humanity have, strangely, been called 'anti-Semitic' as well as the hilariously illogical epithet 'self-hating Jews.' As a Jewish critic of the Israeli government, I have come to accept these accusations as a stamp of approval and a badge of honor, signifying my own fealty to a central element of Jewish identity and ethics: one must be a lover of truth and a friend to the oppressed, and stand with the victims of tyranny, not with the tyrants, despite tribal loyalty or self-advancement. These poems were written as expressions of outrage, and of grief, and to encourage my sisters and brothers of every cultural or national grouping to speak out against injustice, to try to save Palestine, and in so doing, to reclaim for myself my own place as part of the Jewish people." Poems in the original English are accompanied

Fomite
Burlington, Vermont

by Arabic and Hebrew translations.

Roadworthy Creature, Roadworthy Craft - Kate Magill
Words fail but the voice struggles on. The culmination of a decade's worth of performance poetry, *Roadworthy Creature, Roadworthy Craft* is Kate Magill's first full-length publication. In lines that are sinewy yet delicate, Magill's poems explore the terrain where idea and action meet, where bodies and words commingle to form a strange new flesh, a breathing text, an "I" that spirals outward from itself.

Zinsky the Obscure - Ilan Mochari
"If your childhood is brutal, your adulthood becomes a daily attempt to recover: a quest for ecstasy and stability in recompense for their early absence." So states the 30-year-old Ariel Zinsky, whose bachelor-like lifestyle belies the torturous youth he is still coming to grips with. As a boy, he struggles with the beatings themselves; as a grownup, he struggles with the world's indifference to them. *Zinsky the Obscure* is his life story, a humorous chronicle of his search for a redemptive ecstasy through sex, an entrepreneurial sports obsession, and finally, the cathartic exercise of writing it all down. Fervently recounting both the comic delights and the frightening horrors of a life in which he feels – always – that he is not like all the rest, Zinsky survives the worst and relishes the best with idiosyncratic style, as his heartbreak turns into self-awareness and his suicidal ideation into self-regard. A vivid evocation of the all-consuming nature of lust and ambition – and the forces that drive them.

The Co-Conspirator's Tale - Ron Jacobs
There's a place where love and mistrust are never at peace; where duplicity and deceit are the universal currency. *The Co-Conspirator's Tale* takes place within this nebulous firmament. There are crimes committed by the police in the name of the law. Excess in the name of revolution. The combination leaves death in its wake and the survivors struggling to find justice in a San Francisco Bay Area noir by the author of the underground classic *The Way the Wind Blew:A History of the Weather Underground* and the novel *Short Order Frame Up*.

Fomite
Burlington, Vermont

Visiting Hours - Jennifer Anne Moses
Visiting Hours, a novel-in-stories, explores the lives of people not normally met on the page---AIDS patients and those who care for them. Set in Baton Rouge, Louisiana, and written with large and frequent dollops of humor, the book is a profound meditation on faith and love in the face of illness and poverty.

Love's Labours - Jack Pulaski
In the four stories and two novellas that comprise *Love's Labors* the protagonists Ben and Laura, discover in their fervid romance and long marriage their interlocking fates, and the histories that preceded their births. They also learned something of the paradox between love and all the things it brings to its beneficiaries: bliss, disaster, duty, tragedy, comedy, the grotesque, and tenderness.

Ben and Laura's story is also the particularly American tale of immigration to a new world. Laura's story begins in Puerto Rico, and Ben's lineage is Russian-Jewish. They meet in City College of New York, a place at least analogous to a melting pot. Laura struggles to rescue her brother from gang life and heroin. She is mother to her younger sister; their mother Consuelo is the financial mainstay of the family and consumed by work. Despite filial obligations, Laura aspires to be a serious painter. Ben writes, cares for and is caught up in the misadventures and surreal stories of his younger schizophrenic brother. Laura is also a story teller as powerful and enchanting as Scheherazade. Ben struggles to survive such riches, and he and Laura endure.

The Derivation of Cowboys & Indians - Joseph D. Reich
The Derivation of Cowboys & Indians represents a profound journey, a breakdown of The American Dream from a social, cultural, historical, and spiritual point of view. Reich examines in concise!detail the loss of the collective unconscious, commenting on our!contemporary postmodern culture with its self-interested excesses, on where and how things all go wrong, and how social/political practice rarely meets its original proclamations and promises. Reich's surreal and self-effacing satire brings this troubling message home. *The Derivations of Cowboys & Indians* is a desperate search and struggle for America's literal, symbolic, and spiritual home.

Fomite
Burlington, Vermont

Travers' Inferno - L.E. Smith

In the 1970s churches began to burn in Burlington, Vermont. Travers' Inferno places these fires in the dizzying zeitgeist of aggressive utopian movements, distrust in authority, escapist alternative life styles, and a parasite news media. Its characters – colorful, damaged, comical, and tragic – are seeking meaning through desperate acts. Protagonist Travers Jones is grounded in the transcendent, mystified by the opposite sex, haunted by an absent father, and directed by an uncle with a grudge. Around him: secessionist Québecois murdering, pilfering and burning; changing alliances; violent deaths; confused love making; and a belligerent cat.

Views Cost Extra - L.E. Smith

Views that inspire, that calm, or that terrify – all come at some cost to the viewer. In *Views Cost Extra* you will find a New Jersey high school preppy who wants to inhabit the "perfect" cowboy movie, a rural mailman disgusted with the residents of his town who wants to live with the penguins, an ailing screen writer who strikes a deal with Johnny Cash to reverse an old man's failures, an old man who ponders a young man's suicide attempt, a one-armed blind blues singer who wants to reunite with the car that took her arm on the assembly line -- and more. These stories suggest that we must pay something to live even ordinary lives.

The Empty Notebook Interrogates Itself - Susan Thomas

The Empty Notebook began its life as a very literal metaphor for a few weeks of what the poet thought was writer's block, but was really the struggle of an eccentric persona to take over her working life. It won. And for the next three years everything she wrote came to her in the voice of the Empty Notebook, who, as the notebook began to fill itself, became rather opinionated, changed gender, alternately acted as bully and victim, had many bizarre adventures in exotic locales and developed a somewhat politically-incorrect attitude. It then began to steal the voices and forms of other poets and tried to immortalize itself in various poetry reviews. It is now thrilled to collect itself in one slim volume.

Fomite
Burlington, Vermont

As It Is On Earth - Peter M. Wheelwright
Four centuries after the Reformation Pilgrims sailed up the down-flowing watersheds of New England, Taylor Thatcher, irreverent scion of a fallen family of Maine Puritans, is still caught in the turbulence.

In his errant attempts to escape from history, the young college professor is further unsettled by his growing attraction to Israeli student Miryam Bluehm as he is swept by Time through the "family thing" – from the tangled genetic and religious history of his New England parents to the redemptive birthday secret of Esther Fleur Noire Bishop, the Cajun-Passamaquoddy woman who raised him and his younger half-cousin/half-brother, Bingham.

The landscapes, rivers, and tidal estuaries of Old New England and the Mayan Yucatan are also casualties of history in Thatcher's story of Deep Time and re-discovery of family on Columbus Day at a high-stakes gambling casino, rising in resurrection over the starlit bones of a once-vanquished Pequot Indian Tribe

My God, What Have We Done? - Susan Weiss
In a world afflicted with war, toxicity, and hunger, does what we do in our private lives really matter? Fifty years after the creation of the atomic bomb at Los Alamos, newlyweds Pauline and Clifford visit that once-secret city on their honeymoon, compelled by Pauline's fascination with Oppenheimer, the soulful scientist. The two stories emerging from this visit reverberate back and forth between the loneliness of a new mother at home in Boston and the isolation of an entire community dedicated to the development of the bomb. While Pauline struggles with unforeseen challenges of family life, Oppenheimer and his crew reckon with forces beyond all imagining.

Finally the years of frantic research on the bomb culminate in a stunning test explosion that echoes a rupture in the couple's marriage. Against the backdrop of a civilization that's out of control, Pauline begins to understand the complex, potentially explosive physics of personal relationships.

At once funny and dead serious, *My God, What Have We Done?* sifts through the ruins left by the bomb in search of a more worthy human achievement.

Fomite
Burlington, Vermont

Kasper Planet: Comix and Tragix - Peter Schumann

The British call him Punch, the Italians, Pulchinello, the Russians, Petruchka, the Native Americans, Coyote. These are the figures we may know. But every culture that worships authority will breed a Punch-like, anti-authoritarian resister. Yin and yang -- it has to happen. The Germans call him Kasper. Truth-telling and serious pranking are dangerous professions when going up against power. Bradley Manning sits naked in solitary; Julian Assange is pursued by Interpol, Obama's Department of Justice, and Amazon.com. But -- in contrast to merely human faces -- masks and theater can often slip through the bars. Consider our American Kaspers: Charlie Chaplin, Woody Guthrie, Abby Hoffman, the Yes Men -- theater people all, utilizing various forms to seed critique. Their profiles and tactics have evolved along with those of their enemies. Who are the bad guys that call forth the Kaspers? Over the last half century, with his Bread & Puppet Theater, Peter Schumann has been tireless in naming them, excoriating them with Kasperdom....from Marc Estrin's Foreword to Planet Kasper

Made in the USA
Charleston, SC
02 February 2013